Reward of Three

Kelly Jamieson

REWARD OF THREE

ISBN: 978-1-988600-28-4

Cover by Angela Waters
Digital Formatting by Author E.M.S.

Published in the United States of America.

Praise for the Novels of Kelly Jamieson

"Kelly Jamieson delivers a blazing passionate read that tugs at the heartstrings!"

~ **Carly Phillips, *New York Times* Bestselling Author**

"seductive and bewitching from the very start... Softly romantic and wickedly provocative"

~ ***RT Book Reviews* on Rule of Three**

"Kelly Jamieson now has a permanent place on my keeper shelf and I can't wait to see what she writes next."

~ ***Joyfully Reviewed***

"Ms. Jamieson once again gives the reader a richly detailed story that is brimming over with sexual tension, intoxicating desires and intriguing carnal needs that is edgy and psychologically intense..."

~ ***The Romance Studio***

"...I love Kelly Jamieson's books and the way that she depicts her characters..."

~ ***Sizzling Hot Book Reviews***

*This is for Editor Christa – my partner in this book –
thank you for encouraging me and helping me to tell more
of Chris, Kassidy and Dag's story.*

*Also special thanks to Denise Milano Sprung for your assistance
and support for this series – it means so very much to me.*

1

She didn't know how to tell them.

There was the straight-up, open and honest way. There was the sneaky cute way. There was the vague hinting way.

Kassidy wasn't sure if she was any good at sneaky and cute. Maybe if she thought about it enough, she'd come up with an idea. Vague hints might work. But sometimes her guys were clueless. They also weren't always good at subtle. That left straightforward.

But this was a pretty momentous moment. Heh.

In the end, the sneaky cute way came to her like a divine intervention at the most mundane time. Friday nights they often stayed home and watched movies or played board games. Dag had scoffed at the tameness of it all, but as the three of them had settled into their poly relationship, he'd been the first to stretch out on the couch with a beer Friday night and ask what movie they were watching or what game they were playing.

"Scrabble," Chris said tonight.

There was a brief argument between the guys because Dag hated Scrabble. Kassidy sipped her herbal tea and watched them with a smile. Then the Scrabble board came out.

"Man, we're acting more and more like old people," Dag commented, lining up his tiles. "Friday night sitting at home playing Scrabble."

Chris laughed, eyes on his own tiles. "You *are* old. Besides, we're going out tomorrow night."

Kassidy nibbled her bottom lip, her insides fluttering. Was this going to be good news for them? For Dag? If he was worried about staying home on a Friday night, living a staid, boring life…well, this might not be news he wanted to hear.

But they'd talked about it. They'd all agreed. They wanted this.

The game began, and Kassidy glumly surveyed her tiles. She had nothing. She managed to add a couple of tiles to Chris's "ascot" and create "cat". She rolled her eyes. The game continued and then Chris spelled the word "gnat". Kassidy looked at her tiles and the letters P, R and E jumped out at her. Pregnat. Her eyes widened. And then she saw the I and M tiles. Her heart started thumping as she waited for Dag to take a turn, praying he wouldn't touch that word.

He didn't.

Her fingers trembled as she tried to place the little tiles on the board, messing them up, then straightening them. When she drew back, she read her creation: IMPREGNAT.

She looked up at Chris and then Dag. They both frowned at her word.

"That's not a word, sweetheart," Chris said. "You need an E on the end."

"No," she said, "actually I need another N. Right here." She touched the tiles with her index finger. Then she totally cheated by picking up an N from another word and moving it there.

"You can't do that," Dag objected.

She laughed. She'd been so right about the subtle thing. "Oh my God. Read it."

They both looked at the word again and then she saw their faces change at the exact same moment as understanding dawned. They turned shocked eyes to her and she smiled at them. They blinked and in unison, their gazes dropped to her stomach, then back up. She nodded.

"Fuck," Dag breathed. In a flash, they were both kneeling in front of her where she sat on the couch.

"Sweetheart. Really?" Chris gazed at her. "You're pregnant?"

"Yes."

"Fuck," Dag said again.

"Holy shit," Chris said.

They both reached for her and she slid an arm around both their shoulders, bending her head toward theirs. The corners of her eyes stung and she squeezed them shut.

"You okay, babe?" Dag asked in a rough voice that sounded like he was near tears. "Feeling okay, I mean?"

"I feel great."

"When is this gonna happen?"

"According to the website I used, we're due November 9. I haven't been to the doctor yet, but I did two pregnancy tests to make sure."

"You need to go to the doctor!" Chris said.

"I will. I have an appointment next week." She smoothed a hand over his dark gold hair. "I'm fine."

"Wow. November. Okay." Chris swallowed. "Wow."

She tightened her arms around them and they hugged, heads together. "I know. It is pretty wow."

Emotion rose inside her and she felt it in her guys too, their short breathing and vibrating bodies.

"This fucking scares the shit out of me," Dag muttered.

She touched his dark hair. "Why?"

He lifted his head and looked at her, lips pressed together. "It's just…a lot."

She studied him. "Talk to us." She suspected where his thoughts were going. "Wait, get off the floor, both of you."

They rose and sat beside her on the couch, flanking her as they almost always did, on the couch or in bed, or walking down the street. They were always there for each other, but even more, they were always there for her, protecting her, caring for her.

"Why are you scared?" she asked again.

Dag took in a breath. "I never had a dad growing up. My dad didn't give a shit. He took off when I was three. I never had any kind of father figure." He met Kassidy's eyes. "I don't know how to be a dad."

"Yes, you do." She laid a hand on his darkly stubbled cheek. "All you have to do is love our son or daughter. And besides, I don't know how to be a mom."

"At least you had a mom who gave you some kind of good example. Even my mother was a crappy parent. What if I screw up? What if I turn out to be like them?"

"You won't." Chris spoke up. "You're not like them. And Kass is right. None of us knows how to do this. We'll figure it out together. We'll be there for each other like we always are."

They didn't mention the things they'd talked about in the past when they'd considered the decision to have children. They didn't talk about bringing a child into their unconventional relationship. They didn't talk about the kinds of reactions their child might encounter when people learned about their unusual family. They didn't talk about who was the biological father of the baby...because they'd all agreed it didn't matter.

They were all three going to be parents to this baby and genetics didn't change that.

They'd learned a lot from the people they'd met through the counselor they'd seen when starting this relationship. They'd become friends with other poly couples, including some with children. They were fully aware that there were going to be obstacles and hard times. But they were also confident that they could give a child—or two, if Kassidy got her way—enough love and support that their children would be strong and resilient and able to deal with whatever life brought them.

They'd shared their doubts and misgivings, but the desire to have a child and be a family had prevailed and they'd stopped using any kind of birth control two months ago.

Happiness expanded inside Kassidy that it had come to pass, that she was carrying their baby and she was going to give that precious gift to these two men she loved so much.

"What should we name her?" she asked.

Chris and Dag both laughed. "Her?" they said.

She grinned. "It could be a girl."

"You want a girl, babe?" Dag laid his palm on her stomach.

"I'm supposed to say I just want a healthy baby, but I kind of do want a little girl."

"A little girl would be awesome."

"But I really do just want a healthy baby," she added. "Boys can be fun too, and since he'll have two dads, I won't have to worry that I don't know how to entertain him."

"We'll take him to strip clubs," Dag said. "And teach him how to shoot tequila."

Kassidy giggled and gave him a little punch. "Right."

"Hey," he said. "Those are important things in a man's life. Along with hookers, fast cars and guns."

Kassidy stared at him in horror. "Hookers?" Her forehead tightened. "You've never gone to a hooker, have you?"

"Fuck no. I'm kidding, babe. About the guns too. Fast cars, maybe not."

"Oh. For a minute there I was having second thoughts about this."

Dag nuzzled her neck and Chris laughed. "You know he's full of shit."

"November." Dag sighed. "That's not far."

"About nine months," Kassidy said, trying not to smile, and earned herself a tickle.

"Can we have sex?" Chris asked.

"Right this minute?"

His lips twitched. "I meant for the next nine months."

"Christ," Dag said. "Please say yes."

"God yes," Kassidy said. "But even if we couldn't, you two still could with each other. Major benefit of a poly relationship. However, I've already Googled it and learned all about sex while pregnant. Apparently there's increased blood flow to your pelvic area during pregnancy, which can make your genitals swell and heighten sexual sensation."

Dag blanched. "My genitals are gonna swell?"

Kassidy giggled. "I certainly hope so. But no more than usual. Come on, follow along here. *My* genitals may swell."

"Christ," Chris said.

"However, some women report they can't orgasm as easily."

"We'll just have to try harder," Dag vowed.

"Thank you," she said demurely. "I appreciate that. Apparently, many couples find they feel more pleasure from foreplay, oral sex or masturbation than intercourse. So lots of foreplay would be good."

The two guys gave each other evil grins.

"Assuming I don't have morning sickness," she continued. "Because barfing during sex is not, well, sexy."

"Uh…no."

"But it's supposedly important to keep some level of intimacy going throughout pregnancy, to keep the relationship healthy but also to prevent sexual problems after the baby is born."

Chris frowned. "Why would we have sexual problems after the baby is born?"

"Possibly because after I give birth I will not want you to touch me ever again."

Both guys' jaws dropped.

"Kidding! Sort of. Seriously, it might take a while after the baby's born before I'm ready to have sex again—with one man, never mind two! You two could get antsy. But then again, you have each other, which takes some pressure off me." She beamed at them. "This is going to work out great. Not only that—three of us to take turns with diapers and middle of the night feedings."

"Diapers. Ugh." The corners of Dag's mouth turned down.

"You'll be changing your fair share," Kassidy said with a little smack to his shoulder. "Don't even think otherwise."

He groaned, but she caught the soft look in his eyes.

"I'm scared too," she whispered. "This is a big deal, you guys."

"Babe." Dag curled his hand around the back of her neck. "You're amazing. You're gonna be a great mom. The best. Love you so much."

"I love you too, Kass." Chris nuzzled her ear. "He's right. And we're right here with you all the way."

"Th-thanks." She swallowed. She didn't feel much different. Her breasts were a little tender, like around the time of her period. Luckily she didn't feel sick at all. She hoped that continued.

"Speaking of sex..." Dag rose and pulled her by one hand to stand. "Let's go celebrate."

"Mmm. Good idea."

She followed him up the stairs to their bedroom, Chris behind her with his hands on her hips, taking the opportunity to pat her ass. She smiled.

A lamp was on beside the bed, the corners of the room still in shadows. Kassidy loved their bedroom with the king-size bed she shared with her two guys. They'd knocked out a wall between two bedrooms to create this big master suite, with its own bathroom and a small sitting area. With its deep taupe walls, dark wood furniture and softly patterned rugs over dark hardwood floors, it was a place to curl up with a cup of coffee and a book, their own personal space.

Dag turned to face her and Chris pressed into her from behind. Dag lifted her chin with the back of his hand to kiss her mouth. "Kassidy," he whispered.

Chris swept her hair aside and opened his mouth on the back of her neck. Their hands moved over her. The feeling of being between them, of being loved by them, was almost indescribable. She felt so safe and secure, protected and cherished. And sexy. They always made her feel sexy.

She knew how lucky she was. They'd had challenges, but what relationship didn't? She felt so blessed to have these two amazing men in her life, and soon they were going to be even more blessed to have a fourth member of their family, a child who would be so loved.

A hot softness expanded in her chest as she let them pet and kiss her, worshipping her with their hands and mouths. This next stage in their relationship added another, deeper layer to the closeness between them, making it profoundly intimate.

Soon her clothes were gone and they tumbled her onto the bed, joining her there seconds later after they stripped off their own clothes.

She slid down under the covers, shivering a little at the touch of cool cotton on her skin, but when they joined her, their male body heat enveloped her. She sought it out with a shudder of pleasure, letting them sandwich her between their big bodies and continue their petting.

Dag laid a hand on her flat stomach and whispered, "Wow, Kassidy. It's almost hard to believe there's a baby growing in there."

"I know." She smiled and kissed his shoulder.

"Tonight we both have you," Dag murmured near her ear. "Right, Chris?"

Her pussy squeezed and her breathing went shallow. She loved that.

Chris's response came after a short pause. "Right."

But he didn't sound very enthusiastic.

Dag sensed it too. "What?" he asked, lifting his head to look at Chris.

"Nothing."

Dag's eyes pinched. She felt the change in Chris's body, his cock softening against her. She blinked and turned her own gaze to Chris. "What's wrong, honey?"

"Fuck." Chris fell flat on his back on the bed to stare at the ceiling. "It just feels…not right."

She frowned. "What feels not right?"

He didn't answer.

"Chris," Dag said in a low, warning tone. "Talk."

After another pause, Chris said, "She's pregnant."

Kassidy's eyes widened. She glanced at Dag whose forehead was furrowed, then back at Chris.

"Yeah," she said. "I am. So what?"

"It just doesn't seem right to do that…to a pregnant lady."

Dag choked.

Her eyes nearly bugged out of her head. "You have got to be kidding me."

"Sorry," Chris grunted, covering his eyes with one hand. "That sounds stupid."

"I told you it's okay for us to have sex!"

"I know, I know, but…I can't explain it."

"Jesus Christ," Dag muttered. "He's got a Madonna-whore complex."

"What the hell?" Chris moved his hand and glared at Dag.

Now Dag grinned. "Madonna-whore complex. You see

Kassidy as a mother now instead of someone you can fuck."

"I do not," Chris snapped. "I mean I do, but…"

"I've heard of it," Kassidy said.

"I haven't." Chris frowned.

"Freud," Dag murmured. "Men who see their partner as the saintly Madonna can't maintain sexual arousal with her. It feels wrong."

"That's bullshit."

"Is it?" Dag lifted an eyebrow. "You got another explanation for what's going on?"

"Lady in the streets, freak in the sheets," Kassidy murmured.

Dag snorted.

Chris was silent. Then a smile tugged the corners of his mouth. "I'm an idiot, huh?"

"Yeah."

She giggled. "Chris. Seriously? I'm in a ménage à trois relationship with *two men*. Are you kidding me? Yeah, I can be a lady, but how much freakier can you get than this? Don't answer that." She lowered her eyelashes and smiled at him. "I may be pregnant, but I want you to fuck me. Both of you. One in my pussy and one in my ass. How's that for a freak in the sheets?"

Both guys gave strangled laughs.

"Now. Where were we?"

"Need more foreplay, babe?" Dag asked, shifting to kiss her cheek.

She smiled. "I like foreplay. I want to touch you guys too." She stroked over their bodies, warm skin, solid muscles. She found Dag's hard cock and then Chris's somewhat less hard one. She circled a hand around each of them and tugged, eliciting groans from both guys. It wasn't long before they were both equally hard, ready to go, straining against her.

Their thick lengths felt amazing in her palms, throbbing

with male energy. Dag pushed up onto an elbow, leaned over and kissed her hard on the mouth, then kissed Chris. "Who's on top?" Dag whispered.

"Me," Chris said.

Dag eyed him. "You sure?"

Kassidy didn't blame him for asking, after Chris's reaction earlier, but apparently, Chris was over that.

"Yeah." Chris licked his lips. "I'm sure."

They both shifted then and bent their heads to her chest. They kissed her breasts, nuzzled the undersides, then sucked on her nipples. Oh dear God. She was definitely more sensitive there and the firm tugs of their mouths on her shot heat straight to her pussy, making her ache even more. Her hands went still on their shafts as she lost focus, her head spinning, heat rushing through her veins.

Their hands gently squeezed her breasts, plumping them for their mouths, then their teeth in sharp, exciting little bites. A moan climbed up her throat.

A hand slipped between her thighs—Dag's—rubbing over her pussy, just on the outside of it, and she trembled. Then his fingers parted her folds and dipped inside. "Yeah," he groaned. "So wet." His wet fingertips brushed over her clit. Her nerves jumped with delight.

"Mmm."

They fooled around a little more, kissing, touching, Kassidy trying to do more for them, rub their chests, suck their nipples, fondle their balls, but they were focused on her tonight and she had to admit she loved it.

Then Dag rolled to his back, bringing her with him. She stretched out on top of him and kissed him, holding his face in her hands, while Chris moved behind her. His hands caressed her ass and she felt his lips on her there. She smiled against Dag's mouth, Chris's touch spreading tingles all over her body. Then Chris spread her legs, lifted her hips and found Dag's cock.

"Jesus, man," Chris murmured. "Fucking hard as a post."

"You want that?" Dag taunted him.

"You know it."

But they weren't deterred from doing her, and she let sensation wash over her as Chris directed the head of Dag's cock to her opening and helped join them together. She moaned as Dag filled her and Chris's fingers brushed over her clit, then Dag inhaled sharply at Chris's touch on his balls.

They didn't move, Dag pulsing inside her hot and thick, Chris playing with both of them. Then she heard the sound of the lube bottle and as almost a Pavlovian reaction, her pussy melted even more at the thought that Chris was about to take her ass.

He slicked lube over her back entrance and played more, pushing a finger inside her, then two. "Yeah," he groaned.

She loved that added sensation and prepared for an even bigger bite of pleasure when Chris entered her. Her entire body quivered in anticipation and she felt him move behind her on his knees. Then his lubed-up cock pressed against her ass, sliding up and down between her cheeks, tormenting both her and Dag. Dag's arms banded around her, their faces pressed together, their breathing erratic.

Finally, Chris pushed inside her with a ragged moan. Her body jerked and tightened at the flash of fire, but then the sensation of fullness took over. Slowly, carefully, Dag and Chris began to move inside her. Everything was amplified, every feeling exaggerated, every nerve ending electrified, the exquisite dark pleasure almost unbearable.

"Love this," she moaned as they found a rhythm. "Love you. Love you both." Having them both inside her like this, joined so closely, was dirty and hot and sweet. She felt like she was in the center of the sun, burning up, surrounded by heat and light and going up in flames. Hotter. Higher.

They knew how to get her there, so easily, so expertly now, rocking their hips up into her, finding that perfect angle, their cocks creating exquisite friction inside her, their bodies pushing her clit against Dag's body until sensation exploded inside her. She cried out, over and over, their arms and hands tightening on her body, easing her through the fiery beauty of it, and then they came too, maybe at the same time, maybe not. She was dazed and blurry and fighting for breath as their bodies tightened. Dag shouted, Chris groaned.

It was messy and sweaty. Her thighs ached. Her eyes were wet, her hair tangled.

It was perfect.

2

Dag slid out of bed on one side of Kassidy long moments later, dragging a hand over her ass. "I gotta get cleaned up. Wanna come jump in the shower, babe?"

"Mmm. In a minute."

"I'm coming," Chris murmured from her other side. He left the bed too and Kassidy heard the water turn on in the bathroom attached to their bedroom, their quiet voices, then the sound of the heavy glass door on the big shower thunking closed.

She smiled into the pillow, relaxed and satisfied and so very happy. She'd made her two guys so very happy also, and that added to her own joy. She loved giving them this special, precious gift. The baby. Not the ménage sex.

She giggled at her own thought as she lazily rolled over in bed and stretched.

She pushed the covers aside and crawled out of bed, then sauntered across the thick rug toward the bathroom. She paused in the open doorway and let her gaze linger on the shapes of the two men, naked behind the steamed-up glass door. Even though fog obscured her vision somewhat, their bodies were beautiful, Dag's skin a little darker, Chris's muscles a little bulkier. She watched as Dag reached for Chris and pulled him up against him, their mouths joining. When they moved apart, Chris picked up a bottle of body wash and squeezed some into his hands. Kassidy's breath stuck in her throat as Chris reached for Dag's cock and languidly stroked it with both hands. Dag's dark head fell back and one hand flattened on the fogged glass door.

God, that was so beautiful.

She approached the shower, wanting now to join them.

She pushed on the door and slipped into the steamy enclosure, the shower big enough for three they'd had built when they renovated their big master suite after purchasing the house. "Hey, I want in on this," she complained, inserting herself between the men.

Chris grinned down at her, his eyelashes dark and wet, water running over his sleek shoulders. "Just washing him up, sweetheart. You can come between us any time."

Dag's hands landed on her waist and his lips touched her shoulder. "Yeah. What he said."

The three of them began to wash each other, slick, soapy hands everywhere, Kassidy giggling at a ticklish touch or a nip of lips on her neck.

"So, Chris," Dag murmured. "You over your Madonna-whore complex? Or do I get Kass all to myself for the next nine months?"

"Shut the fuck up," Chris said mildly. He cupped one soapy breast. "I just had a moment."

Kassidy giggled. "It was kind of funny."

Now Chris gave her wet ass a little slap and she jolted, laughing again. "Hey!"

"You laughing at me?" he growled, leaning in and kissing her lips.

"With you, big guy," Dag said. "We're laughing *with* you."

"It was an understandable reaction," Kassidy added.

Chris's lips curved up and his eyes gleamed. "No way

in hell I'm going nine months without having sex with you, sweetheart."

"Glad to hear that." She wound her arms around his neck and pressed her wet body to his. Behind her, Dag's hard, slick body pushed against her butt and as Chris cupped her face in his hands, slanted his head and came in for a deeper kiss, Dag's arms went around both of them to Chris's ass. "Very glad to hear that."

"When are we going to tell people?"

Chris looked up from the newspaper he was reading at Kassidy's question. Saturday morning they lounged around in the great room attached to the kitchen, drinking coffee—well, Dag drank his usual Coke—reading the newspaper and checking sports scores on TV. "Aren't you supposed to wait a while?" he asked.

"Yeah. Most people wait until the first trimester is over. In case there are problems. I guess once you're past that, it's more likely you won't lose the baby."

"Okay, so we wait three months," he said.

"I can't wait that long!" Kassidy cried.

Chris exchanged a grin with Dag.

"Babe," Dag said. "It's not that long."

"It is!" She sighed. "Okay. I can wait to tell people at work." She and Chris worked together at RBM Technologies. "Acquaintances. But I can't wait to tell my parents. And our friends." She gave them big brown eyes that pleaded with them.

As if they could say no to her.

"Sweetheart, if you want to tell them, that's fine," Chris said cautiously.

"What's the point of waiting?" she demanded. "If something goes wrong, we're going to tell them then anyway. It's not going to make dealing with it any easier."

"True that." Dag nodded. "Let's just tell the world then."

"No. We don't need to tell everyone. Um, we didn't talk about what we'd tell people...you know, people at work, or acquaintances. They're going to assume the baby is Chris's." She bit her lip.

Dag nodded. "Yeah. I know that." He shrugged. "It doesn't matter what people think. All that matters is what we think. And we know that our baby is going to have two fathers."

"I love you, Dag," Kassidy said softly, reaching for his hand to squeeze it. He smiled at her and Chris's heart gave a kick against his ribs watching them. Yeah, that kind of sucked. Lots of people still thought he and Kassidy were a couple and had a friend living with them. They'd been pretty open about their relationship with some people, but not everyone. There were some people who just didn't need to know. But if things had been reversed, Chris wasn't sure how accepting he'd be of people assuming the baby was Dag's when it was just as much his.

"Are you going to tell your parents?" Kassidy looked at Chris from beneath her eyelashes.

His mouth twisted. "Well, I have to tell them at some point."

"I mean, are you going to tell them now?"

Anxiety torqued in his gut. "Can't see that going well."

"They're going to have a grandchild," Kassidy said softly. "They would want to know about that, wouldn't they?"

"I'll think about it." He looked away as an awful thought entered his head. He and Dag and Kassidy had agreed it didn't matter who the biological father of the baby was, because they were both going to be fathers to whatever children they had. But his parents...if it wasn't their biological grandchild, would they be interested in the baby at all? Would they insist on knowing before they'd have anything to do with the baby? Or were they so done with him and his unusual family that they'd have nothing to do with *any* grandchild?

He'd thought he'd come to accept that his parents were never going to be part of his life again because of his choices, but this was telling him that he *hadn't* completely accepted it. Because having a child was a big thing, and he found he wanted his parents to be involved. He wanted them to see him as a father, to see him raising a child with his partners. He wanted his kid to know his—or her—grandparents.

"I'll call Mom and Dad and invite ourselves over for Sunday dinner," Kassidy said with a grin. "We can tell them tomorrow. Maybe Hailey will come too."

"We can tell the gang tonight at Cole and Tyra's place," Dag said.

"No!" Kassidy stared at them wide-eyed.

"Uh, thought you *wanted* to tell them," Chris said.

"We can't tell them before my parents!"

"Oh. There's a hierarchy, is there?" Dag asked.

Kassidy wrinkled her nose. "Well, yes. Obviously you have to tell family first."

Chris met Dag's eyes and they exchanged another amused glance. "Okay. Fine. We'll tell them some other time. Although people are going to wonder why you're not drinking tonight."

"Oh. Yeah." Her forehead furrowed. "I can hide that. I think. Or I'll tell them I'm not feeling well."

"We have a designated driver for the next nine months," Dag said with a smirk.

Kassidy threw a cushion at him. He caught it and laughed. "Actually probably longer," she said. "I won't be able to drink much while I'm breastfeeding either."

"Huh. Breastfeeding. Right."

Kassidy did manage to conceal her no-alcohol status

from their friends that night without arousing suspicion, although Chris and Dag both kept an eye out and distracted people a couple of times.

"Nine months of no drinking," she grumbled on the way home.

"Maybe Chris and I should quit drinking too," Dag suggested. "In solidarity."

"Jesus, seriously?" Chris demanded.

Dag laughed. "I can do it."

"You don't have to do that," Kassidy said. "Although that's very sweet. But maybe on weekends we won't have a bottle of wine with dinner like we usually do. Would that be okay?"

"Whatever you want, sweetheart," Chris said. "We're here for you. All the way through this."

"Mom! Don't cry!"

Kassidy moved around the guys to get to her mom and hug her.

"How can I not cry?" Mom sniffled and squeezed Kassidy tightly. "You're going to have a baby. Oh my God. That's so wonderful."

Then Kassidy started crying too and hugged her mom back.

"Jesus," Hailey said. "You'd think she was the first person to ever have a baby."

Kassidy lifted her head and looked at her sister, who grinned and held out her arms. "C'mere."

Kassidy smiled and moved to her sister and they hugged too. "As usual, you're the favorite," Hailey said, her voice sounding choked. There would have been a time when this comment would have pissed off Kassidy, but now she knew Hailey was teasing. Sort of.

"I'm not the favorite," she protested mildly. They'd been through all this before. At one time Hailey had seriously believed that.

"Sure you are. You're giving them their first grandchild."

"I'm the oldest."

They both gave sniffly laughs.

"You're going to be a great mom," Hailey whispered. Kassidy drew back and Hailey looked at Dag and Chris. "You guys ready for this?"

"Christ, no," Dag muttered, but he forced a grin.

Kassidy caught the shadows that crossed her mom's face and the way her gaze went back and forth between Chris and Dag. Mom was genuinely happy for them, she knew it, but was also concerned.

Guess that wasn't a surprise.

Dad now moved in for a hug. "That's awesome news, Kassie," he said, kissing her forehead. "Guess you can call us Grandma and Grandpa now."

They chatted about due dates and the baby's room and maternity leave while they ate dinner, but Kassidy made sure that wasn't all they talked about. Hailey's business as a mixology consultant was growing, and Kassidy wanted to hear more about that.

After dinner, Kassidy helped her mom serve dessert in the kitchen. "Are you really happy for us, Mom?" Kassidy asked quietly, sliding a piece of cheesecake onto a plate.

"Of course I am." Mom bit her lip. "But I am worried. A bit."

"About…?"

"About how this is going to work." Mom sighed. "I don't want to be negative about it. You know I love Chris and Dag both. You three are beautiful together, and even though it's unconventional and we had misgivings, you seem to be making it work. How long has it been?"

"Three years." Kassidy paused. "What misgivings?"

Mom lifted one shoulder. "Just whether you were doing the right thing."

"You never told us that," Kassidy said quietly.

"Of course not. Would it have made any difference? It only would have made you angry at us. Distanced you from us."

Kassidy looked down at the caramel sauce she was about to spoon over the cheesecake. "Yeah. You're probably right. That's basically what happened with Chris and his parents. Now they barely talk."

"We didn't want to be like that."

Kassidy wrinkled her forehead as she looked back at her mom. "Did you feel the same way they did?"

"No. Of course not. Although at first we didn't realize that Chris and Dag were in love too."

"Does that matter?"

"No." Mom gave her a reproving look. "That doesn't matter. Not to us. But it does complicate things. Chris's family's reaction...well, everyone's different. I'm not going to criticize them for their beliefs. Ours are different. I *can* criticize them for not accepting their own son though. We wanted to support you because we love you no matter what, and we definitely wouldn't want to lose you because of the life you chose."

Mom picked up two plates. "But naturally we had misgivings. About how others would judge you. Would it impact your career? Or Chris's? And now, baby. A child who's going to grow up facing those same barriers. A child with two fathers—how will he or she explain that to kids at school? To teachers?"

"You know, when I went to school, there were lots of kids who had three parents. Or four. Blended families. Remember Allison Danez? Her parents divorced but they still got along, even when they both remarried. They all participated in their kids' lives. There were lots of parent-teacher conferences where all four parents were there. Or Christmas concerts."

"That's not quite the same."

"I know it's not exactly the same, but I do think most teachers will accept that three parents isn't that unusual. We don't need to share every detail of our lives with them."

"Well, that's just one example of the kinds of challenges you all will face."

"We know that." Kassidy lifted her chin. "We talked about it a lot, Mom. We know there will be challenges for our children because of our family. We've already faced some of those." Her mouth twisted a little. "But we think we can overcome those challenges and raise a son or daughter—or maybe both—who is strong enough to deal with them too."

Mom smiled. "In some ways, I couldn't be prouder of you, Kassie. It takes a lot of strength to forge your own path when it's outside the norm."

Kassidy shrugged, but her throat thickened. "I don't feel like I'm doing anything that special. I just feel so lucky that I have both Chris and Dag in my life. That they love me. We are really, really lucky in so many ways. That's what we have to focus on."

"And that's also why I'm proud of you. Come on. Let's get this cheesecake out there."

Dag arrived at his office Monday morning, greeted his assistant Jami, helped himself to a cold Coke from the fridge in the small kitchen/break room, and waved at his small staff as he passed by the open cubicle area on the way to his office.

Holy hell, he had fucking huge news to tell them! He was going to be a father.

But he couldn't say anything yet.

With the success of his new venture a few years ago, he'd had to rent office space and hire staff. He was glad the business was doing well, but this was starting to become like the nine-to-five kind of job he hated. The rush of excitement at starting something new and the thrill of taking a risk had diminished, but he was still enjoying building the company. In fact, they were waiting to hear back from a client in Australia, a huge company who was looking at implementing their online training package. That would be their biggest sale yet, and they'd had some big ones.

In his office, he cracked open the Coke as he started his computer.

A father.

Never had he imagined this for himself. His life had never been easy. As he'd become an adult, he'd tried to deal with his feelings for Chris by screwing around with anyone who'd have him, men and women, both at the same time. When he'd never found anyone he cared about as much as Chris, he'd pretty much resigned himself to being single—and therefore childless—forever.

Now he had two people in his life he loved and who loved him back. People who knew all those dark, ugly places inside him and loved him anyway. And there was going to be a third. A tiny little person.

Christ, that scared the shit out of him.

He both longed for it with a deep, unrelenting ache, and feared it.

He tried to focus on e-mails but it was not happening. For a few moments, he let his thoughts slip away, remembering Kassidy's face as she'd told them she was pregnant. Or let them read it on a fucking Scrabble board. His lips curved into a smile. A hint of uncertainty had shadowed her eyes though, as if she wasn't sure if she was sharing good news or bad.

Of course it was good. It was fucking *fantastic.* It was the best news.

But he was still terrified.

A tiny person who would depend on him for everything, whose life would be molded by everything he said and did. The potential for an epic screw up was so real, he felt panic start to buzz in his brain and his stomach go queasy.

He had to remind himself that he wasn't in this alone. He had Chris and Kass. He drew in a few long, slow breaths to try to control his racing heart. They'd be there for him. They wouldn't let him screw up. He wouldn't destroy some innocent child's life by being the worst father in the history of fathers.

He would focus on the good things. The fun he and Chris would have taking the little dude to ball games. Or dudette. Because girls could like baseball too.

And Kassidy's parents had been nothing but supportive. Their unconditional love for him was another bright spot in his life that he'd never anticipated. Despite their misgivings about their relationship, they had faith that he could do this.

When Kassidy had talked about waiting to tell other people in case she lost the baby, he'd tensed up. He didn't even want to hear those words "lose the baby". As if he wasn't fucking terrified enough. The only thing that scared him more than *having* a baby would be *losing* the baby.

Okay. Business. He had work to do.

He opened his e-mail and started clicking through. He scanned his inbox to prioritize and saw the e-mail from The Curbow Group in Australia. He hovered his cursor over the e-mail, then clicked it open. His eyes widened and a smile broke out on his face as he read their message. They were offering a contract.

Holy, holy shit! This was fanfuckingtastic!

He read the e-mail once more to make sure he wasn't

hallucinating due to the stress of impending fatherhood, but no, it was true. He leaped up from his desk and strode out of the office to share the news with his team.

They were all as ecstatic as he was. Everyone had busted their asses on this proposal. Fist bumps and high fives were exchanged along with a lot of jubilant laughter. It was too early to celebrate with drinks, but they'd definitely do that after work.

Then realization struck Dag with a cold fist—he was going to have to go to Australia to get this set up. Realistically, this was going to take at least a few months, possibly as many as six. And the plan was to start in late March. He'd be gone for most of Kassidy's pregnancy.

But, even worst-case scenario, he'd be back before the baby was born.

That sucked. He wanted to be here for every minute of it, to make sure she was okay, to share all this with Chris and Kassidy. How could he leave now?

How could he not?

His mind started sorting through options, but there weren't many. He could take one of his staff, in fact he'd *need* to take someone with him, but there was no way anyone else could handle this project.

Back in his own office, he let out a harsh sigh and set his lips together. Timing was everything. They'd done away with birth control a few months ago and he hadn't even been thinking about how this would work if they got this contract. Shit.

Well. They'd just have to deal with it the best they could. But he was not looking forward to telling Kassidy and Chris he was going to be gone for that long while she was pregnant.

3

At her own office Monday morning, Kassidy found herself bursting with the news she so desperately wanted to share. They'd agreed not to tell people at work. But she'd been working on this project for the last month, working closely with an external consultant, and the more she thought about it, the more she felt she should tell him. Their go-live date for the new sales force management system was December first, and chances were, she wasn't going to be there then. That was crappy timing, but what could she do? A knot of guilt formed inside her about that.

Jeez. They'd picked her to work on this project and she'd been thrilled, but now she felt like she was letting them down. Her career was important to her. She wanted to do well at her job and at this project. This was a great opportunity to show them what she was capable of. The manager of Human Resources at RBM was retiring next year and Kassidy had entertained the idea that she would really like that job.

But she was having a baby. How was that all going to work?

In her cubicle, she sighed. Having a baby was complicated, even in a "normal" relationship. She'd heard of women taking maternity leave and losing their jobs. Or being passed over for promotions. No wonder so many women took a short leave of absence. Of course, many couldn't afford to take longer off work. She luckily wouldn't have that problem. But still, she didn't want to lose her job or lose out on opportunities because of this.

She got up and walked down the aisle to the cubicle where Damon Orr had his temporary space. He worked for the company RBM had hired to implement the new sales force management system. He was managing the project and she was working closely with him to develop the training their staff would need to use the new system. She was leading a small sub-team working under her on that part of the project.

Kassidy paused at a cubicle. "How are you feeling, Lissa?"

Lissa had called in sick on Friday.

"Better," Lissa assured her. "Much better. Thanks for asking."

Kassidy looked up and saw Damon standing at his own cubicle, smiling. "Morning, Kassidy."

"Good morning," she said, approaching him. Damon moved into his cubicle and gestured at the extra chair for her to have a seat. She sat and he moved around to the chair behind his desk.

Damon Orr was a good-looking man, no doubt about that. When he'd started working with them, she'd been expecting some computer geek with horn-rimmed glasses and no social skills. Nothing like getting sucked into stereotypes. Instead, he was six feet tall with a lean, wide-shouldered build, short dark hair, the perfect amount of designer beard stubble and expensive suits. He did wear glasses, but they were stylish frames that made him look very sexily smart. He was also very charming, with a great sense of humor.

"You're really good with your team," Damon commented, sitting in his chair.

She smiled. "Thanks." She crossed her legs and tugged her skirt a little lower on her thighs. Damon's eyes dropped briefly to her legs. "Lissa doesn't miss time very often. I was hoping she'd be in today."

"So, what's up?" Damon's beautiful brown eyes behind his stylish glasses lifted and focused warmly on her face.

"Well. Um." She swiped her tongue over her bottom lip, then tried to ignore how Damon's glance had flicked to her mouth. "How was your weekend?"

"It was okay," he said, leaning back in his chair. "Nothing exciting. How about you?"

This was the kind of question she'd dealt with every day for the past three years. She couldn't be completely honest, so her answers were all superficial and misleading. It was starting to wear on her—the deception, the feeling that this all devalued her relationship with Chris and Dag. "It was good. Went to some friends' place Saturday night. Had dinner with my parents yesterday." True…but not entirely.

She didn't mention that she had two boyfriends. Everyone at RBM thought she and Chris were a couple. Some knew Dag lived with them, but assumed it was just a convenient arrangement. Dag didn't give a shit. Most of the time. She and Chris both squirmed with discomfort at this sometimes, but they'd agreed this was the best for their careers. There'd been times it had been not so great for all of them, even Dag—the company Christmas party the last few years, for example, a few other social functions Chris was expected to participate it as a VP of the company, and the time one of his co-workers had invited them to his wedding.

Sometimes Kassidy thought it would be better if people knew the truth. But then she thought about how people would react. Always in the back of her mind was what had happened to her friend from high school, Steve, how he'd been beaten up coming out of a gay bar, bad enough to put him in the hospital. How she'd overheard some guys at work talking about a gay colleague who'd come out, their ugly words making her heart hurt. What if they said those things about Chris and Dag? And she thought about what had happened to some of their other poly friends—some people got all paranoid because they thought they were looking for more partners to swap, or thought that poly meant cheating, and you couldn't trust a cheater. And she backed away from the idea of telling everyone.

She would so like to live in a world where people didn't have to pretend to live their lives in a way that was acceptable to everyone, when they weren't hurting anyone.

"I worked," he confessed with a sheepish smile.

"Damon! You work way too many weekends. And evenings."

Actually they'd both worked a lot of late nights lately, getting the project started. If this was any indication of how things would go when they got closer to deadline, she was even more worried about how that was going to work being nine months pregnant.

What had she gotten herself into?

"Eh," he said with a shrug. "Got nothing else going on."

She already knew he wasn't married and had no girlfriend, although he did seem to have a fairly active social life. When he wasn't working, that was. No doubt a good-looking, smart, successful guy like him had no trouble finding women to go out with.

"Well, you should," she said firmly. "You need to have fun sometimes."

"I have plenty of fun." He winked at her.

She smiled. She liked Damon. They got along great, had similar ideas about how to manage their teams. She liked how he consulted her and involved her, but was perfectly willing to cut to the chase and make a tough decision when needed. They'd spent a lot of time working together and had taken coffee breaks and lunch breaks together numerous times. He was easy to talk to and they'd shared some of their personal lives with each other.

But this was just a business relationship and even though she felt guilty about the fact she was going to leave him hanging in the wind when she left, she resisted the urge to tell him about her pregnancy and assure him that she'd do everything she could to make sure her leaving the project early caused no problems. "So. This morning we have a meeting to start brainstorming some training strategies."

"Yeah. Nine o'clock. I'm going to get Starbucks—want something?" He pushed up out of his chair with easy masculine grace. Today he wore a gorgeous charcoal suit with a dark shirt and lighter gray tie.

"No, thanks." She'd already learned caffeine was something else she was going to have to limit. "See you at nine."

She returned to her cubicle. Before her meeting, she typed up an e-mail to her best friend Danielle about getting together after work one evening for drinks so she could share the news with her. Ha. Except she'd be drinking a virgin margarita while Dani tipped back martinis. Ah well. Kassidy rubbed her stomach. It was all worth a little sacrifice for the sake of Belly Bean inside her.

She smiled. She had no idea where that name had come from, but she liked it. Belly Bean.

She and Danielle ended up going out the next evening, meeting after work at a casual restaurant near Kassidy's office. Dani raised her eyebrows when Kassidy asked for water when the waitress arrived to take their orders. "Water?" she asked.

"Sure." Kassidy smiled at her. "You have a drink if you want."

"Eh." Dani shrugged. "I don't need a drink." She looked over the menu. "I am hungry though."

"Me too. Starving." Kassidy paused. "I guess that's what happens when you're eating for two."

"Yeah." Dani's eyes moved on the menu, then her head snapped up. "Wait, what?"

Kassidy grinned.

"Eating for two?"

Kassidy nodded.

"You're *pregnant*?" Dani screeched.

"Yes."

"*Omigod*!" Dani jumped out of her chair and rounded the table. Kassidy rose and they hugged tightly. Kassidy ignored the interested glances from other patrons in the restaurant. Her heart fluttered with happiness.

"That's amazing, Kass." Dani pulled back and smiled at her. "I'm so happy for you."

"Thanks."

They sat again. The waitress came and took their orders.

"I'm happy for me too," Dani said, smiling. "I get to be an aunt. Sort of."

"Auntie Dani," Kassidy agreed. "Sounds perfect. We're going to tell the rest of the gang this weekend, but I wanted you to know first."

Danielle smiled. "Can I help you decorate the baby's room?"

"Probably. Somehow I don't think Dag and Chris are going to be that interested."

Dani frowned. "They are happy about this though, aren't they?"

"Oh yeah! Dag's nervous. He's worried about being a

good father. Chris is..." She hesitated, not sure if she really wanted to tell Danielle about Chris's odd reaction in bed that night. He'd been fine since. "Chris is really happy."

"Good."

"But guys aren't into all the baby stuff and decorating."

"No, probably not. Well, we'll have fun. Let's go shopping this weekend."

"Awesome."

Kassidy's doctor appointment on Thursday confirmed the pregnancy and confirmed her due date as November ninth, and that she was healthy. Dr. Fortney was unfazed by the fact that Kassidy was accompanied by two men—Kassidy had told her about the relationship, confident that she wouldn't judge her.

She decided to plan a dinner party that weekend to make the announcement to their friends. She carefully planned the menu, her cooking skills having improved considerably since she and Chris had moved in together. Dag enjoyed cooking too, and often it was the two of them preparing meals together.

This was one way their individual relationships had developed—they liked doing different things together, not always all three of them. Kassidy and Dag liked shopping for food and cooking; Dag and Chris liked baseball and football and going to the gym; Chris and Kassidy liked talking shop, since they worked for the same company, and trying out new restaurants, and they all liked going to movies together.

She got Chris setting the table and lighting candles in the dining room while she and Dag prepared roasted potatoes with lemon and oregano, roasted asparagus with feta, Chicken Souvlaki and a big Greek salad.

Cole and Tyra arrived first, then Matt with his girlfriend Olivia, then Brandon and Danielle, who came together but were "just friends" and finally Jeff and Sarah. Sarah came in all flustered. "Jaden was having a tantrum because we were going out without her," she said. "Oh my God, I need a big glass of wine."

"Here you go." Dag handed her a glass of red with a grin.

"You should have brought her," Kassidy said. "She could come."

"She'd be the only kid here," Sarah pointed out, taking the glass. "Thanks. Besides, it's nice to have an adults-only evening once in a while."

This would all be different a year from now. Jaden wouldn't be the only child because she and Dag and Chris would have a baby. Cole and Tyra had been together for a while—when were they going to start a family?

They all sat in the living room with a fire going in the fireplace, music playing on the stereo. Dag and Chris handed out drinks, and Kassidy flitted back and forth between the living room and the kitchen, checking on last minute things, and bringing out bowls of olives, hummus with pita chips and some feta puffs she'd made earlier.

They made their announcement once they'd all sat down to dinner. Dag did it, with a formality that made Kassidy's heart squeeze. She watched the love and pride on his face as he told everyone she was pregnant, and then she looked at Chris and saw the same emotions on his face and once again she knew how truly blessed she was. Both men looked at her and she smiled.

Everyone erupted in congratulations and toasts were made, Kassidy participating with water in her wine glass.

"Are you ready for how much your life is going to change?" Sarah asked. "All your freedom and independence? Gone. You won't even be able to go to the bathroom alone for the next six years."

Kassidy giggled. "Oh no."

"Seriously," Sarah continued. "You're going to breastfeed, aren't you? Jaden nursed every two hours for the first four months. Even at night. I've never felt so trapped in my life, not to mention exhausted."

Kassidy glanced at Chris, then Dag, who were both faintly frowning. "Well, we'll deal with it," she said lightly.

"Even when they get older, it doesn't get much easier," Sarah continued. "Whole days would go by and I hadn't even brushed my teeth. Sometimes it takes all day to do a load of laundry because I can't get back to it. It feels like I do laundry every damn day."

Kassidy blinked.

"I'm sure it's stressful at first," Danielle said warmly. "But I'll be there for you. And you have two great guys to help out."

Kassidy smiled at her friend. "True."

"I've been planning my trip for this summer," Danielle announced, and Kassidy was grateful for the change of subject. "I'm thinking about Australia."

Danielle loved to travel in the long summer vacations she got as a teacher.

"No shit?" Dag said. "I'm going to be there this summer."

Kassidy straightened. "What? You're going to Australia?"

Dag's face changed, a strange expression crossing it, then going blank. "Um. Yeah. I, uh, didn't tell you about that yet."

"Because of that big contract you just got?" Chris asked.

"Yeah." Dag looked down at his plate. "I'm going to have to go there to help get things set up for our client."

Kassidy's insides squeezed. "Oh. Wow. Australia. That's cool. When will that be?"

Dag met her eyes and gave a small smile. "Let's talk about that later, babe."

She pursed her lips, questions flowing into her head. "Okay. Sure." She looked at Danielle. "Well, that'll be an awesome trip."

4

"Why didn't you tell us?" Kassidy sat in the middle of the bed, her silky brown hair around her shoulders, knees to her chest, arms wrapped around her legs. She wore her pink and gray polka-dot flannel pajama bottoms and a long-sleeved pink T-shirt.

Dag sighed. *Shit.* "I'm sorry, Kass. I was going to tell you, but not like that. That slipped out."

Chris pulled his shirt over his head and tossed it toward a hamper. When it landed on the floor, Kassidy frowned at him.

"When were you going to tell us?" she asked. "And how long will you be gone?" Her eyebrows sloped down. "You'll be here when the baby is born, won't you?" Her voice actually quivered.

Dag climbed onto the bed and set his hands on her shoulders. He looked her in the eyes. "Yes," he said emphatically. "I will be here when the baby is born. No matter what. I'm going to have to be gone for a while and it sucks, but nothing will keep me from being here when the baby comes."

"How long will you be gone?"

He grimaced. "Not sure. Could be six months."

"Oh my God!" Her eyes widened. "*Six months*? Seriously?"

"Holy shit," Chris muttered, retrieving his shirt and dropping it in the hamper.

"I know." Dag rubbed his forehead. "I'll try to make it as short as I can. And I can probably swing a few short visits home. I'll have to leave sometime at the end of March or early April."

Her eyes got glossy as if she was going to cry and she blinked rapidly. Shit. "I'm sorry, Kass. So sorry. The timing sucks. But this is a huge contract and nobody else can handle it."

She nodded, her smile shaky. "I know. But I'm going to miss you."

"Me too." Chris joined them on the bed. He gave Dag a hard look. "That is a long time to be away, man. Especially now."

Shit, now they were both mad at him. He fucking hated that. He swallowed a sigh. What else could he do? Sell the business? Eventually he probably would, but he needed to make it worth something before he could sell and walk away, like he'd done with the last business he started. That business had been worth millions; this one couldn't be worth that much yet.

Kassidy sighed. "Danielle and I bought some baby things today. Do you want to see them?"

The guys exchanged a look then said, "Sure."

She gave a crooked smile. "They're in the baby's room."

"You've already decided which that is?" Dag moved off the bed.

"Yeah. The one next door."

They had four bedrooms. The one across from their room was a guest room, although they rarely had guests from out of town. Chris's parents had never visited them since they'd bought the house. The other rooms had minimal furnishings.

They all went into the room and Kassidy flicked on the light. "We need to get a crib," she said. "And other furniture." Dag nodded, even though his chest felt tight. She unfolded a quilt she'd bought and held it up. "I didn't buy the whole set in case you don't like it." Dag glanced at Chris, who studied the quilt, and his chest tightened even more. "It's gender neutral," she continued, running a hand over the pictures of cute monkeys and giraffes in shades of yellow, light green, beige and turquoise.

"It's great, Kass." His voice came out rough.

"I was thinking we could paint the walls this shade of yellow. You can get all kinds of matching accessories," she continued. "Curtains, wallpaper, a mobile. And look." She picked up a stuffed animal. "Danielle bought this monkey for the baby. It matches. Isn't it sweet?"

The sight of her holding that stuffed monkey with its goofy smile damn near sent him to his knees. "It is. C'mere." He pulled her against him then slung an arm around Chris's neck to yank him in too. "I'm sorry, baby, I really am. I don't want to go."

"I know." She pressed her face into the side of his neck, sliding one arm around his waist, the other around Chris. "But it'll be fine. Pregnancy isn't that exciting." She drew back and made a face. "You'll miss me getting all fat and waddling."

"I want to see you waddle," he said. She frowned. "Er, let me rephrase that. You won't waddle. And you won't be fat. You'll be round and beautiful. And I am going to miss that so fucking much."

Fuck, fuck, fuck. He pressed his lips to her forehead and closed his eyes.

He'd never before had to make choices or sacrifices like this. He'd lived his life the way he wanted. Yeah, he'd been selfish. He'd never cared enough about anyone to have to make tough choices. He worked hard, played hard, and even after he and Chris and Kassidy had come together, he'd pretty much sailed along. He'd learned to compromise for them. And he hadn't minded it at all. But now, business was taking him away from something so goddamn important he felt a bitter resentment rising inside him.

This was what having a family was.

This was new to him. And the fact that it pissed him off so much was a little scary, because it meant he cared. He cared a helluva lot. He swallowed, his jaw tight, hand on the back of Kassidy's neck, holding her against him.

"You two mean more to me than anything," he murmured. He turned his head and pressed his forehead against Chris's. "I mean that."

"I know," Kassidy whispered.

Chris grunted.

"And our baby. The baby means more to me than anything too."

"Belly Bean."

He went still then choked on a laugh. "Belly Bean?"

Kass lifted her head and met his eyes, hers shining. "That's what I've been calling him or her. Until we know."

Chris laughed too. "Damn, Kass."

Dag smiled, his heart swelling so huge. "I like it."

"We'll be fine, Dag," Kass said softly. "I know you're torn up about this, and none of us like it. But we'll be fine."

"Yeah," he murmured. "We will."

Sunday night Chris called his parents.

He'd debated for the last ten days whether or not to tell them. In the end, he knew he had to. He could wait. He could even wait until the Belly Bean was born. Not that he'd be procrastinating if he did that. There was something to be said for having a living, breathing baby to show them that they were now grandparents.

But they might *not* be grandparents. Biologically. Genetically.

Why was this bugging him so much? He and Dag had agreed it didn't matter who was the biological father. Chris totally bought into that. This was his kid. His and Dag's.

But every time he thought about his parent's reaction, he knew, he just fucking *knew* they were going to have an issue with that. And that was why he'd hesitated about calling them.

Dammit, he wanted them to know.

Why did it matter so much to him? They hadn't disowned him, whatever the hell that meant. They still talked, although not often. They hadn't visited since that night three years ago when they'd discovered their son was in love with another man. And a woman. But they hadn't completely cut him off, so there was that.

He'd tried to visit them, but he wasn't going there without Kassidy and Dag, and they weren't having that, so it hadn't happened.

He hated their reaction. He hated that they wouldn't accept Kassidy and Dag and him being together. And yet, it still made him sad. They were his parents.

"Okay, gonna do it," he announced to Kass and Dag. Kass sprawled on the couch with a bowl of popcorn—Christ, she'd been eating all weekend—and Dag sat at the other end with her feet on his lap, both of them watching TV.

"Do what, honey?" Kass asked, dipping her hand into the bowl.

"Call my folks. Wish me luck."

Both their heads snapped around to look at him.

"Okay, man, good luck," Dag said slowly.

"That's good, hon," Kassidy said firmly. "You need to tell them."

He nodded and touched the screen of his phone to call their number.

He got his dad and made some stilted small talk with him for a few minutes. Finally he said, "Is Mom around?"

"Yeah. You want to talk to her?"

Chris wasn't sure which parent was better to make the announcement to. Probably his mom, but since his dad had answered the phone, he'd go with that. "Just wanted to know if she's around. I have some kind of big news for you, you'll want to tell her." Would she want to talk to him when she heard?

"Okay. What's your news?"

"Kassidy's pregnant."

There. It was out.

Silence.

"Oh," Dad said slowly. "Really?"

"Yeah, really." He shot Kassidy and Dag a brief smile. "She's due in November."

After another pause, Dad asked, "Who's the father?"

Chris pressed his lips together. He'd known that was coming. "Dag and I are," he said firmly. "Both of us."

More silence. Then he heard Dad relay the news to Mom. There was a brief, hushed conversation between them he couldn't hear, then Mom came on. "Chris? Is this true?"

"Yeah, Mom. You're going to be a grandma."

"Oh." The word was a sigh. "But..."

"I know what you're thinking," he said, making it easy on her. "We don't care who the biological father is. We're both going to be a father to the baby. I'm gonna be a dad."

He heard a small noise, like a hitched breath.

"I'd like you to know your grandchild," he said quietly. "I hope you'll come visit when he or she is born."

This time he definitely heard a sniff. "I...I..."

Then Dad came on the line again. "Chris. Your mom's upset." He heard the accusing note in Dad's voice.

"I'm sorry," Chris said evenly. "That wasn't my intention. I just wanted you to know about this and have an opportunity to know your grandchild."

"I have to go. Your mom's crying."

"Yeah. Go see to her. That's fine, Dad. Bye."

He ended the call with a tap of the screen. He looked at Kassidy and Dag. "Well. As I expected. That didn't go well."

Kassidy shifted her legs and set down the popcorn. "C'mere."

He sat on the couch between them. Kassidy leaned her head against his shoulder and Dag set his hand on his thigh and squeezed.

"It's their choice," Dag said, voice rough.

"Yeah."

"They have nine months to come to terms with it," Dag added.

"Well, technically, only about eight," Kassidy put in. "But still. Maybe they'll come around."

Chris sighed. "Whatever." He didn't even want to hope that could happen. He hadn't realized the faint hope inside him that they would react positively to the news, until they hadn't, and disappointment had crushed that dream in a brutal fist. "What are you guys watching?"

"*Sons of Anarchy.*"

He settled back and stared at the TV as if watching, although for the next fifteen minutes he kept replaying the short conversation with his parents and getting more and more annoyed, especially at his dad. Chris had been hoping for happiness and instead Dad got angry because he'd upset Mom.

Shit.

He was finally letting go of it, getting distracted by the TV show, when his cell phone rang.

He grabbed it and saw it was his parents. "Christ," he grumbled. "Now what?" He debated letting it go to voicemail, then answered it. "Hey."

"Chris? It's Mom." Her voice sounded a bit thick but strong.

"Hi, Mom." He sensed Kassidy and Dag's curious looks.

"Chris. I'm sorry. I got emotional when we talked earlier. I wanted to call you back and tell you that's wonderful news."

He blinked. "Really?"

"Yes. We talked about it. Your father's…concerned."

"I get that."

"Well, we both are. But…a baby."

"Yeah." His own voice went gruff.

"You're going to be a dad."

"Yeah."

"We didn't know if that would ever happen. How you would handle that. I guess I don't really want to know the details of your private life, but I want you to know, we're happy for you. Having a child is a precious gift."

"Mom." Christ, now *he* was getting choked up. Growing up, he'd known his mom had loved him. He'd thought his dad did too, although Dad had been a macho, tough guy who hadn't tolerated weakness or failure, hadn't expressed a lot of emotion. For the last few years Chris had questioned the extent of their love for him, given their inability to accept his relationship with Kassidy and Dag. But now…maybe they did love him. "Thanks," was all he could squeeze through his tight throat.

"We'll talk more. Keep us posted about how things are going. Kassidy's feeling okay? She's healthy?"

"Yeah. She went to the doctor this week. Everything's good."

"Can I talk to her?"

He inhaled sharply and looked at Kass. "She wants to talk to you," he mouthed.

Her eyes widened. Then she nodded and held out her hand. He handed her the phone.

"Yes, thanks. Yes," she said, eyes fastened on him.

"Folic acid? Yes, the doctor recommended a good prenatal vitamin that has iron and folic acid." She paused. "A little tired. And hungry all the time." She smiled. "These days they say about twenty-five to thirty-five pounds is good."

Chris looked at Dag with raised eyebrows. Jesus. Mom was bonding with Kassidy over this baby. Who would've fucking thought?

If his dad would come around…wow.

"Thanks, I will. Bye, Kathy."

Kassidy ended the call and carefully set the phone on the table. "She's really thrilled," she said slowly. "Oh Chris."

Her arms came around him from the front and he turned to bury his face in her neck. Dag's hard body pressed up against his back in a three-way hug. They sat like that for a long moment while he got control of his violent, tumbling emotions.

"Guess she really wanted to be a grandma," he finally said, separating them. He smiled at them both. "Who knew?"

Over the next weeks, they bought baby things and planned and dreamed the future of their baby and their family. And life went on—Dag planned his trip to Australia, Chris and Dag hit the gym and kick boxed, Kassidy got deeper into her project at work. They worked out, played Scrabble, tried new recipes and read about what to expect when you're pregnant.

One Thursday night, Kassidy and Damon were still working at six o'clock and wanted to get the presentation they were doing for the executive leadership team the next day completed before they left for the day. They probably had another hour or two of work.

"I'll order in food," Damon said.

"Okay," Kassidy agreed. "I'm starving."

"What would you like? Pizza? Sandwiches?"

"How about both?" She grinned. "Kidding. Anything's fine with me."

"I'll order a pizza. Pepperoni and mushroom okay?"

"Um, could we skip the pepperoni?" She made a face. Normally she liked it, but for some reason now even the smell of it made her stomach turn. As did sausages and bacon, which was weird because she *loved* bacon. However, when it came to dill pickle potato chips, she could eat bags of them at one sitting. *Bags* of them. She craved them all time.

She kept tapping at her laptop keyboard, sitting at a long table in one of the meeting rooms on her floor. Through the glass windows she could see all the empty cubicles. Everyone else had gone home.

Damon used his cell phone and was talking into it when Chris appeared.

"Hey, Kass."

She looked up at him in the open door, all big and golden with his wide smile. "Hi." She smiled back.

Everyone knew they lived together, but they didn't get physically demonstrative at work. But right then she wanted a hug. She was tired and her neck and shoulders had tightened into rocks, which meant a headache was coming.

"We're going to be a while," she said. She tilted her head toward Damon. "He's ordering pizza for us."

Chris's smile slid off his face. "Kass. You've been working late every night this week."

"I know." She grimaced. "It's got to get done. I want this to go well." Also there was the guilt that she wasn't going to be there to see the project through to completion.

"I'll take the train home," she said. "No worries."

His eyebrows lowered. "I do worry," he said quietly. "It's cold out. It's late and you're…"

She nodded. "I'll be fine," she said firmly. "We'll get done as quickly as we can."

She could see he didn't want to leave her there.

Damon ended the call. "There we go. Half an hour. I let security downstairs know. They'll call me when it gets here. Hey, Chris. How are you?"

"Not bad," Chris clipped. He eyed Damon with unhidden displeasure.

Damon dropped back into the chair next to Kassidy and leaned closer so he could see her laptop screen. "Now, where were we?"

Kassidy bit her lip and looked at Chris. His face had tightened, his square jaw stony.

"Sorry, honey," she said, using a rare endearment in the office. "I'll be home as soon as I can."

"I'll wait," Chris said tersely. "I'll be up in my office. I have some things I can do. Call me when you're done." He gave Damon a long, hard look then turned and walked down the corridor back to the elevators.

"Shit," Damon said in a low voice. "Did I piss him off? Don't want one the VPs mad at me."

Kassidy shook her head. "Don't be silly. Besides…" she grinned, "…you've already got this contract."

"True that." He gave her a crooked smile back.

"He's just protective," she added.

"Yeah. Well, I don't blame him. If you were my girlfriend, I'd be protective too." His smile was slow and warm.

Ah…she didn't know where to go with that. "So. We need to put these last slides in a different order. And there are still some points we need to add about risk assessment."

"Yes, ma'am." He nudged her shoulder with his and they got back to work.

It was just past seven-thirty when they decided they'd done enough. The empty pizza box had been pushed to the end of the table, after Kassidy had devoured most of it, along with a bunch of empty water bottles. Kassidy stretched her hands above her head, then rotated her neck.

"Holy God, my head hurts," she said with a sigh. "My neck is killing me."

"Why didn't you say something?" Damon rolled his chair behind her.

"We were trying to finish."

"Shit, Kassidy, you should have told me you needed a break."

"I'm fine," she said. "Just tired. I'll probably go home and go straight to bed." She rubbed her neck.

"I give pretty good massages." He set his hands on her shoulders. She froze at first, but then his fingers dug into the tight muscles, quickly finding all the sorest spots that made her moan.

"Oh wow. You *are* good at that..." She bowed her head and let him work the muscles. She knew this wasn't really appropriate, but damn, her head throbbed and it felt so good. So she let it continue for a few minutes before lifting her head, pushing her hair back and moving away. "Thanks. Feels better already."

"Good. Want you back here tomorrow for the presentation to the executive committee."

"I will totally be here." She reached for her cell phone and sent Chris a text telling him she was ready to go. "Good night, Damon."

"Night, Kass."

5

Chris sat at the boardroom table on the twelfth floor, surrounded by the executive management team—him as Vice President of Product Development, CEO Ron Carlisle, Chief Financial Officer Jennifer Halsey, Daksh Agarwal, VP of Human Resources, VP of Operations Donovan Smith and their General Counsel Lois Danford. They were all watching Kassidy.

Well, Kassidy, Damon Orr and Takako Himuro, VP of Marketing, the project sponsor. Chris narrowed his eyes a little at Damon Orr. The guy was good looking, charming and smart. And he was spending a lot of time with Kassidy.

It wasn't that Chris didn't trust Kassidy. It was just, he couldn't imagine any guy being around Kassidy that much and not falling for her a little. Or a lot.

Eh. He was being stupid. He focused on Kassidy standing at the head of the table, holding the remote control for the computer that was playing her PowerPoint presentation on the wall to her left, relaxed and comfortable. "Change management will be an important part of the training structure," she said. "And to be successful, change has to involve people, not be imposed on them. We want to involve staff as much as possible in the development and implementation of the new system.

When we communicate the vision for the company with the new system, when we share what we want to achieve to become a market leader, we can inspire people to move and make changes. We'll need to have the right people involved, people with the right skills but also the right emotional connection. People with positive attitudes and enthusiasm. We know RBM can be the best, and we want our entire team to believe that and to communicate that urgency and passion to everyone in the organization."

Christ, she had not only him engaged, but everyone else at the table. He'd never been so proud of her.

Well, okay maybe he had. Accepting his feelings for Dag, falling in love with Dag herself and being so open to the kind of relationship they all had—that was pretty incredible. Carrying their baby—that was even more impressive. This was…this was just *her*, doing her job, and doing it fucking amazingly.

Something expanded in his chest and he smiled as he watched her. The rest of the leadership team were nodding enthusiastically, and he thought Daksh was about to break into applause.

When they'd finished and Kassidy and Damon had left, Tak Himuro sat down. "Well?" Tak said to the rest of the team. "What do you think?"

"I think this project is in good hands," Ron said. "They said everything I wanted to hear. Answered all our questions. Their project charter is sound."

"They nailed the deliverables," Donovan added.

"Their timeline is ambitious," Jennifer noted. "But somehow I feel confident they can meet those milestones."

Nobody yet knew Kassidy was pregnant. The loose silk blouse she wore hid the tiny bump that had recently appeared. Nobody knew she wasn't going to see this project through to the end, but she and Chris had talked about it and he had confidence in her too, that she would do everything she could to make sure the project would not be set back by her early departure.

Ron glanced at Chris with a wry smile. "You want to add anything to that?"

Chris grinned. "That woman is brilliant."

They all laughed. "We just saw evidence of that," Daksh said. "She's got a great future here."

Chris nodded, once again pride and love filling his chest. He couldn't wait to get Kassidy home and tell her what a great impression she'd made on everyone. And then get her into bed and celebrate.

Fuck yeah.

"Oh sweet Jesus," Kassidy groaned. Dag was working on giving her a second orgasm of the night, after Chris had had his turn at her pussy. He'd been hot and desperate for her, voracious but gentle, carefully laying her on the bed, the two of them taking their time stripping her out of her clothes, kissing and tasting her everywhere. Dag had sucked her tender nipples and caressed her breasts while Chris went down, then, when she was limp and breathless, they changed places.

Now Dag flipped her over onto her stomach and lifted her hips into the air. She gasped as he nipped at her ass cheeks, then buried his face in her pussy from behind and used his lips and tongue to make her entire body quiver and shake. When his tongue flicked over her sensitive clit, her body jerked.

Chris petted her back, kissing his way slowly from nape to the base of her spine, opening his mouth there in a long, sensual kiss. His tongue then drew a hot path back up her spine until he kissed her neck again, sucking on her skin with gentle yet possessive pressure.

Dag caressed her ass, her thighs. Her entire body bloomed with pleasure, quaking with bliss, heat rolling over her. She gasped and clutched the sheets in fists, then collapsed into a trembling, sweaty heap on the bed, hair over her face. She pressed her knuckles to her mouth. "Wow," she breathed.

"Wanna fuck you so bad," Chris murmured, stroking her hair with one hand and his own cock with the other. He was swollen and flushed, heavy veins pulsing.

Dag grabbed Chris, one hand on his face, and turned Chris toward him for a long, hard kiss. She watched them through her orgasmic haze, and her pussy started tingling again with need. Their mouths and tongues moved together for long moments, Dag's hand sliding down Chris's jaw to the side of his neck, then lower to rub over a nipple. Chris groaned, head falling back.

Dag gave Chris a little shove and he fell on his back next to Kassidy. Dag proceeded to kiss his way down Chris's ridged abdomen. He laid a kiss on one square hip bone, buried his face in the crease of his groin, then turned and mouthed Chris's hard cock.

With one of his hands still on her lower back, Chris grabbed Dag's hair in the other and pulled, directing Dag's mouth where he wanted it. "Yeah," Dag murmured as he took Chris into his mouth.

"Fuuuuck," Chris groaned. "That feels good."

Dag took him deep, sliding his mouth up and down Chris's shaft, and Kassidy watched with a growing ache between her legs.

Then Chris gave Dag's hair another tug and pulled him off him. "Stop," he gasped. "Too close."

"Just wanted to make sure you're ready," Dag said with a smirk.

"Oh, I was ready."

"That's good," Kassidy purred. "Because I need you to

fuck me. Now." Just saying the words made her tummy do a little flip.

Chris rolled and moved over her, nudging her legs apart with his knees. He held her hip and stroked his cock up and down through her swollen and slick flesh.

"You come up here," Kassidy said to Dag. "I want to suck you while he fucks me."

"Sucking and fucking," Dag said. "If that's what you want, I'm in." He knee-walked over the bed and propped some pillows against the headboard, then sat and positioned himself in front of Kassidy's face. She went up on her elbows and reached for him. The solid shape of his prick filled her palm and she curled her fingers around the base. She took her time, studying the smooth head, the thick, rigid maleness. Then she lowered her head and kissed the tip.

She let her tongue flick out in a teasing caress, then swirled it around the crown. Dag's hands filtered through her hair, letting strands slide between his fingers, and then he fisted handfuls of it. The tingles from her scalp ran all down her spine.

She was brimming with sensation, Chris behind her, teasing her pussy into an unbearable aching need while Dag tugged her hair and she filled her mouth with him. She savored the erotic tang of Dag's clean taste, the scent of his skin, the weight of him on her tongue. And she relished the pleasure noises they both made, deep, rough, male sounds.

"So hot, watching you suck him off," Chris said. He pressed against her entrance and she moaned around Dag's flesh as he penetrated her. "Hot. Tight. Fuck." Chris eased in deeper, out a little, then back in, filling her, stretching her with delicious pressure.

"Her mouth is hot too," Dag murmured, holding her hair off her face and watching her with brilliant eyes. She held his gaze as she opened her lips and slid them down his wet shaft. She took him as far as she could, but Dag was big. She used her hand to help, keeping her eyes on his even though her body burned and throbbed. Her other hand slipped beneath his balls and cupped them with gentle pressure. They maintained that eye contact, intense, intimate and erotic. Dag's beautiful face wore a flush, his eyes went heavy-lidded and his tongue wet his lips. "Oh fuck yeah. You know what I want."

She did. With utmost care, she let her teeth scrape over him, then paused and held his cock in a light bite, gently setting her teeth against firm flesh. He sucked in air between his teeth, his hands tightening in her hair, then groaned.

She released him to tongue his balls, exploring the thin, soft skin, the puckered seam, then continued to suck his cock while Chris slid in and out of her in a slow, dreamy rhythm. Heat spiraled through her, every nerve ending electrified, her senses dazzled, and her head went a little light. Chris skimmed a hand over her hip, around to her belly, down to her pussy to find her clit.

"No. Wait," she gasped. She held Dag's cock and looked over her shoulder at Chris. "I want to make him come first."

Chris gave her a wicked grin. "Go for it, sweetheart. Wanna watch him come too. Then I'll make you come so hard."

"I'm close," she admitted. She turned her attention back to the stiff prick in her hand and the dirty smile playing on Dag's lips.

"Make me come, babe. Suck me good. Yeah, like that."

Dag's eyes fell closed and Kassidy let her own flutter shut, turning herself over to the sensation that assaulted her from every direction. Dag's hands held her head and his hips lifted, fucking up into her mouth, never too hard or too deep, never hurting her, just taking what he needed and in doing so, giving her what she needed too.

"Aw, Kass," he moaned. "There it is…gonna come…now…"

She lifted off him, barely, letting the tip of his cock rest on her tongue as he pulsed. His balls contracted in her hand and the taste of his semen filled her mouth. She loved that. Loved giving him that, loved…him.

She licked him again with tender strokes of her tongue, swallowing his taste and savoring it, exploring the texture of his skin.

"Christ, Dag," Chris gasped, going still. "That was hot…watching you come. I'm close too…"

Dag shifted back a little into the pillows and Kassidy rested her face on his thigh. Releasing him, she slipped her hand down beneath her and found her clit. Her inner muscles quivered and tightened, a hot coil of need building. Dag's hands played in her hair, gentle now, sensual and sweet.

Her whimpered noises got louder, faster, as flames built to a sharp shimmering peak of ecstasy. She cried out as she came, shuddering, tightening around Chris inside her as he pounded into her, hands hard on her hips. He was right there with her, growling out his own release, going taut and still, pulsing inside her.

"Jesus, Kass," he panted.

She smiled against Dag's thigh, fighting for breath, her pussy pulsating with tiny aftershocks, her tight muscles letting go, her body going lax and boneless. "Mmm. Thank you."

Dag rolled over in bed the next morning, reached for Kassidy's warm body and found cool sheets. He lifted his head. Chris slept on the other side of the bed, the covers at his waist, revealing the muscular wedge of his back. Dag peered at the alarm clock. Seven-fifteen. Huh. That was early for Kassidy to be up on a Saturday.

He heard noises in the bathroom. He'd heard pregnant women had to pee more often—was that starting already?

He closed his eyes and smiled at the intimate nature of his thoughts. They'd been living together three years now and there wasn't much that was secret from each other. Any of them. Poor Kassidy, with two guys knowing every detail of her menstrual cycle and leg-shaving routine.

He drifted a little, in and out of sleep, happy it was Saturday and they could laze around in bed. Fool around in bed. Yeah...

When he next opened his eyes, the clock said seven-thirty.

He frowned and rubbed his eyes. Was she still in the bathroom?

He flung back the covers, ready to go look for her when the bathroom door opened and she appeared. Wearing her plush pink robe, she held a hand to her stomach. She approached the bed and he caught a glimpse of her pale face in the light from the bathroom.

"Dag," she whispered. "Are you awake?"

"Yeah, babe."

"Something's wrong."

He sat up. "What? What's wrong?"

"I'm...b-b-bleeding."

His eyes went wide and his heart stuttered. "Jesus, what?"

She nodded, her bottom lip trembling, her eyes shining with tears. "I don't know what's happening."

"Fuck. Let's get you to the doctor." Unease shifted in him, cold and tight.

"It's Saturday."

"The hospital then." He reached across and gave Chris's shoulder a shove. "Chris. Get up. Now."

"What the fuck?" Chris mumbled, rolling to his back. He frowned at them in the dim morning light.

"Kassidy's bleeding," Dag snapped. "Get up and get dressed." He was already out of bed and pulling on a pair of boxer briefs, then jeans. "Kass, sit down."

He moved her to the chair. Her whole body was trembling and the worried look in her eyes made his gut contract painfully.

Chris shoved out of bed too. "What? Kass, honey..." Naked, he strode around the bed to crouch in front her. "Are you okay?"

She blinked wet eyelashes at him. "I don't know."

"What happened?"

"I had some cramps yesterday. A bit of spotting last night. After you fell asleep. I was a little worried, but I thought it might be because we had sex. Then I woke up this morning with worse cramps and I-I felt I was wet." She bit her lip briefly. "I went to the bathroom and discovered I'm bleeding."

Chris closed his eyes briefly then squeezed her hands. "It'll be okay, sweetheart."

Her lower lip quivered again.

Chris jumped up to look for clothes. "Kass, you need to get dressed," he said. "What can I bring you?"

"I-I don't..." She looked around. "My yoga pants right there. And a hoodie."

Dag went to the closet for a hoodie. "Underwear?" he asked.

"Um. Just a bra. I have panties on. I had to u-use a pad."

Fuck. Dag gritted his teeth as he found a bra and then they helped her dress.

"I'll carry you downstairs," Chris said.

"I can walk," she protested.

"Are you in pain?"

"The cramps are pretty bad," she admitted.

"Shit." He bent and picked her up and headed to the stairs.

Dag drove to the hospital with reckless speed, Chris sitting in the back with his arm around Kassidy, her head tucked against his shoulder. He heard her murmur, "Belly Bean," her hand on her abdomen, and in the rearview mirror he saw Chris's face go stark with pain.

He pulled up outside Emergency in a designated spot and was out of the car before the engine had even died. He yanked open the door. Chris climbed out, helped Kassidy out then picked her up again.

"She's pregnant," Chris announced at the counter, holding her in his arms. "And bleeding."

Dag found a wheelchair and brought it up as they answered endless questions that made him want to shout, "For fuck's sake, get on with it! She could be losing our baby!" Then they took her back to an exam room, but as Dag and Chris followed, they were stopped by a short, stocky nurse. "Who's the father?" she demanded.

They looked at each other, then back at her. Together, they answered, "We both are."

The nurse frowned.

They stared her down.

"Fine," she muttered, with a shrug. "You can both go back."

They rushed down the corridor to find her. Kassidy was already lying on a stretcher and a nurse was covering her with a sheet. "How far along are you, honey?" the nurse asked.

"Ten weeks," she whispered.

She looked so pale and scared, which was exactly how Dag felt as he moved to her side. Chris joined them. The nurse proceeded to take some blood. "The doctor will see you soon," she said as she left.

"I need to change the pad," Kassidy whispered, looking

up at them with big terrified eyes. "I can feel I'm soaking through."

"Jesus." Dag swallowed down his fear. "I'll go ask for something."

He was well past being embarrassed about any damn thing, and he strode out to find someone and ask for another pad for Kassidy. The nurse frowned and came back with him. "Let's have a look," she said, pulling the curtain to shield Kassidy from them.

Dag and Chris met each other's eyes. Much as Dag hated that fabric barrier, he didn't know if he could bear seeing Kassidy bleeding. What was happening? If it was that much blood, that was not good.

Chris reached for his hand and they stood close together and wrapped their fingers around each other tightly as they waited. Something hard pulsed in his gut. They could hear the murmured voices of the nurse and Kassidy.

"Can't believe this," Chris muttered. "Goddammit."

"I know. I know." Dag gripped Chris's hand, both of them hanging on to each other. He wanted to repeat Chris's assurance that things would be okay—but he was too afraid they weren't. "Just want her to be okay. Is that terrible to say?"

"Hell no." Chris swallowed. "But I'd like the baby to be okay too."

"Yeah. I'm worried about Belly Bean too. But if anything happened to Kassidy…"

"She'll be fine." Chris squeezed his hand. "She's strong and healthy."

The nurse drew back the curtain and left, and they both rushed to Kassidy, one on each side of her. Tears streaked her cheeks, dampening her hair. They each grabbed a hand. Her fingers felt cold and small as she curled them around Dag's hand.

"It's really hurting," she said in a low voice. "Like really bad cramps."

"You should have something for the pain," Chris said.

"The nurse is getting me something."

"Good."

Fuck! Dag felt like his heart was being ripped out of his chest, his entire body hurting. Seeing her in pain and crying and bleeding was fucking killing him. He'd never felt so helpless and he hated it.

"It's gonna be okay," Chris said again. Dag wasn't sure if Chris really believed that, or just didn't know what else to say.

"No, it's not," Kassidy sobbed. "I'm so scared, you guys. Our Belly Bean. Oh *God.*"

Dag's eyes burned as he lifted her hand to his mouth and pressed it to his lips.

"We're here with you, baby," he said. "Whatever happens. We're here."

They waited for what seemed like forever for a doctor to come. Chris and Dag got chairs and pulled them up beside her bed, holding her hands, wiping her tears, giving her sips of water. Dag studied the tightness at the corners of Chris's mouth and eyes. This was fucking awful.

When the doctor showed up, a kid who looked like he was still in high school, he asked the same questions all over again. Dag held on to his patience with a tenuous grip. The doctor then said they'd do an ultrasound. He didn't say she'd lost the baby. He didn't say anything encouraging either.

The medication helped Kassidy's cramps some, but she continued to cry silent tears that broke Dag's heart. He could see Chris struggling too, trying to hang on to his own fears to reassure Kassidy and keep her calm as they waited.

Finally, they took her for the ultrasound.

"Can we come too?" They both stood.

The same nurse gave them another look but nodded, and they walked as the nurse pushed Kassidy in the wheelchair.

In the dark room, the technician squeezed globs of gel onto Kassidy's stomach that had just started to round out a little, then started moving the transducer over her skin, all the while studying the screen. Nobody said anything. Since they had to stand on Kassidy's left, they both held her left hand. And each other's.

Finally, the technician stopped and put away the transducer. "I'm sorry," she said. "The doctor will be here in a moment."

Fuck! What the fuck did that mean—she was sorry? Dag and Chris turned to stare at each other.

Kassidy's sob sliced through Dag like a knife.

The doctor came in then, looked at the ultrasound results with the technician and turned to them. "I'm sorry," he repeated, looking like he wanted to run. "The ultrasound didn't find a heartbeat. I'm afraid you've lost the fetus."

6

A few hours later they were on their way home. Kassidy had painkillers and instructions to see her doctor the next week. She stared out the car window as Chris drove. Dag insisted on sitting in the back with her, trading places from the trip to the hospital. He slid his arm around her, but she kept her face turned away from him.

She wasn't crying anymore. She probably had no tears left in her. But her entire body hurt, pain radiating from her throat through every limb, anguish squeezing her lungs.

She wasn't pregnant anymore.

She'd only barely come to believe she really *was* pregnant. It hadn't seemed real at first, despite the positive tests and the doctor confirming it. But then she'd known. She'd felt it. She'd felt the differences in her body, the fatigue, the hunger, the cravings, and the smells and tastes that repelled her. She'd put on a little weight. Her breasts felt fuller and tender. Belly Bean had become real.

Could Bean really be gone?

"Maybe the ultrasound was wrong," she said suddenly.

Chris's head jerked and Dag's arm tightened around her.

"Maybe they didn't look hard enough," she continued. "We should go back!"

"Ah, Kassidy." Dag pulled her head down to his shoulder.

She didn't want to believe it. She wanted to believe it was a mistake and Belly Bean was still growing inside her.

Her eyes stung, but no real tears came.

When they got home, Chris and Dag were solicitous. "Do you want to lie down?" Chris asked her. "Come on. Let's go get you into bed."

"I am tired."

Once they'd gotten her changed into pajamas and in bed, Dag said, "Hungry, babe? I can make you something to eat."

She rolled her head back and forth on the pillow. "No. Not hungry."

They sat on the bed on either side of her. Neither seemed to know what to say or do. And neither did she. She closed her eyes. "What did I do wrong?" she asked them in a weary voice.

"God, Kass." Chris shifted closer. "You didn't do anything wrong!"

"Fuck no," Dag added.

"I must have done something wrong. I don't understand why this happened. We were so happy."

"Nobody knows why these things happen," Dag said quietly.

"I was working a lot," she whispered. "I'm so sorry."

"Kass. Kass, please don't apologize." Chris's voice sounded choked. He pulled her into his arms. "Please don't apologize. This is not your fault."

She wanted to blame someone. She wanted there to be a reason this had happened. She wanted to understand it. And the only one to blame was her.

"Kassidy, baby." Dag rolled up against her and his arms came around her and Chris. "Don't even think that."

They were all silent for a long time. Then she said, "How will we tell people?" Thinking about telling her parents made her want to cry all over again. Except she was too exhausted to cry, tired and hurting right to her bones. And telling Dani and their friends... She let out a long shaky sigh.

"We'll tell them," Chris said. "Dag and I." His voice came out thick again.

She gave a tiny nod.

"We'll do anything you want, baby," Dag said, stroking her arm. She felt his kiss on her hair. "Anything. Love you so much."

Her heart hurt so much she couldn't even say the words back to him. It felt like pain and grief had squeezed all the love out of her. She didn't want to feel anything anymore.

"I want to sleep," she mumbled against Chris's chest.

"Sure, honey." They moved away from her, tucked her in and left the bed. She thought they were going to leave her alone, but after they moved around the room, they joined her in bed. She really just wanted to be alone. They were trying to comfort her, but she felt pressured. She needed time. She didn't know how to tell them that. So she just went to sleep.

She was sleeping a lot.

Chris's insides knotted. He and Dag kept checking on Kassidy all day Sunday. She didn't want to get out of bed. She didn't want to eat. She wasn't crying anymore, but the obvious despair she was feeling ate at both of them. What could they do? There was nothing they could do to make this better for her.

Or for themselves. They didn't talk about it, but Chris himself was struggling with emotions. Guilt. What if the sex they'd had Friday night had caused the miscarriage? He found himself in front of his computer Googling causes of miscarriage. Sex was supposedly safe. That couldn't have been it. But it felt like such an awful coincidence that the miscarriage happened right after they'd done it.

So yeah, he felt guilty. But he also felt angry. Why had this happened? They didn't deserve this. They'd been doing everything right. Kassidy took care of herself. Working long hours wouldn't be the reason; she was crazy to blame herself. But then, he was probably crazy to blame himself too. There was no explanation for what had happened.

They procrastinated on calling family. It wasn't going to be easy. And when Chris thought about calling his parents, a dark wave of misery swamped him. His mom had been so happy. It seemed like this might be the thing that could bring them back together. What did that mean now?

The answer to that was too painful to even think about.

This was so not fair. So *fucking* unfair.

He slumped in the chair in front of the computer in the den, pressing the heels of his hands to his eyes. Anger simmered hot inside him.

"Chris. You okay?"

Chris lowered his hands and straightened at Dag's voice behind him. "Yeah. Sure." He spun the chair around and studied Dag. Man, he'd never seen Dag look like that. The guy never let on that he gave a shit about anything. Or he never used to, anyway. When it came to him and Kassidy, Dag's hard edges had softened. Still, with others, he gave off that I-don't-give-a-shit vibe. Now his mouth was tight, his eyes full of pain, his body tense. "What about you?"

Dag shrugged. "I'm okay."

They both nodded, looking at each other, then looking away.

Fuck.

But there was no point in all three of them falling apart. That wouldn't do any good.

"We have to make some phone calls," Dag said.

Chris squared his shoulders. "Yeah. Let's get it over with."

He rose out of the chair and they walked out, going to find their cell phones.

"I don't even know how to do this," Dag said moments later in the living room.

"I remember when my grandma died," Chris said quietly. "My mom sitting at the kitchen table phoning all the family members to tell them. She had a list of people she had to call. Telling them the same thing, over and over."

"Christ." Dag closed his eyes, his face drawn into stark lines of unhappiness. "I guess it's the same, huh? Someone did die."

"Yeah," Chris agreed quietly. "Someone did die. We have to hold it together though."

"I'm not gonna break down and cry," Dag said with annoyance.

Chris shook his head, one corner of his mouth lifting. "Never said that. C'mon." He laid a hand on Dag's shoulder. "I'll call my parents. Obviously." His gut clenched at that. "And Kassidy's parents. You call Jeff and Sarah, Tyra and Cole. Call Danielle and ask her to call the others."

Dag eyed him. Clearly, he knew he had more calls to make, but he also knew Chris's were going to be the worst. "Okay."

They made their calls. He kept his shit together. Said the terrible words. Kassidy's parents were coming over. His parents were not. Of course. They were too far away. But they were disappointed too.

Disappointed? Was that *really* the word to describe how

wrecked he felt? Probably not. But whatever. He could handle this.

Not only were all his hopes and dreams about being a father gone—so were his hopes and dreams about having his parents back in his life, accepting his family. It was something so raw and painful he didn't even want to go there. He pushed that away.

He dropped his cell phone to the couch cushion beside him and listened to Dag talking in a low, quiet voice. "Yeah," Dag said. "She's okay. I mean, she's really upset, obviously, but physically she's okay. They gave her pain meds." He listened. "Yeah, thanks, man. Means a lot. We'll talk, yeah?" Dag nodded then ended the call. He too slumped back into the couch. "Holy shit. I think that was the hardest thing I've ever had to do."

"Other than watching Kassidy while she went through that."

Dag's eyes squeezed shut. "Yeah. Fuck yeah. Seeing her in pain like that…so miserable. Christ."

Chris rolled his head on the couch to look at Dag. "C'mere." He reached out a hand and grabbed Dag's, then gave a yank. Dag came into his arms easily. They needed contact. Physical closeness. Kassidy was up in the bedroom, wanting to be alone. They wanted to give her space, let her have time to deal with this. But Chris wanted Dag next to him.

They sat together in the quiet house, arms wrapped around each other, until Kassidy's parents arrived.

Hope walked in and went straight into Chris's arms. He hugged her. Then she turned to Dag and hugged him too. Chris took in the look on Dag's face, Hope's affection for him almost making everything worse. He still wasn't completely used to having people who cared for him like Hope and Dave did, the family he'd never had.

Chris met Dave's grave eyes and nodded. "Dave. Thanks for coming."

Dave nodded too. "How's Kassie?"

"Not great. She's upstairs."

"We'll go see her up there," Hope said.

Chris and Dag followed along behind as they climbed the stairs. Hope went straight to the bed where Kassidy lay huddled beneath the covers. She touched Kassidy's hair. "Hey, sweetie, we're here."

Kassidy's eyes fluttered open. "Mom. And Dad." Then her eyes filled with tears.

"Oh baby, it's okay." Hope sounded choked as she sat on the bed and pulled Kassidy into a hug. "Kassie, sweetie. I'm so sorry."

"I know," she choked out. "Me too."

"There's not much more to say, is there?" Hope said softly. "We're all sorry. Nothing can fix this."

Dave stood there, jaw tight, hands in his pockets, staring at the floor. Poor guy. Dave probably felt like he and Dag—hating to see their girl hurting like that, helpless to do anything about it and uncomfortable with the violent emotions.

Kassidy let her mom rock her and stroke her hair. Dave approached the bed and laid a hand on Kassidy's leg over the covers. "We're here for you, Kassie. Whatever you need."

"Thanks, Dad."

"What can I do for you, sweetie?" Hope drew back. "Should I stay and make dinner?"

"I'm not that hungry."

Hope smiled. "Maybe not, but your two guys might be. I'll get something together for them."

Truthfully, Chris wasn't that hungry either, but they needed to eat and Hope needed to do something to help.

"D'you want to come downstairs?" he asked Kassidy. "You can sit in the kitchen and watch."

She looked like she was going to say no, but without much of a change of expression she nodded and pushed the covers back. Dag went straight to her and slid his arm around her waist. "Okay, babe?"

Chris moved nearer too, ready to carry her if need be.

"Yeah." She stepped away from both of them and walked out of the room.

They went down to the kitchen and settled Kassidy on a stool at the island while Hope bustled around looking in the fridge and cupboards. Dag showed her where a few things were. Dave turned on the TV in the attached family room and found a hockey game.

"Do you want to talk about it?" Hope asked Kassidy.

She shrugged.

"When did it start?"

"Friday night. A bit. Then I woke up Saturday morning bleeding."

Hope nodded. "You went to the hospital right away?"

"Yes." Kassidy related some of the details, her voice going shaky. Then she stopped talking.

"You will be okay," Hope said gently, leaning on the island to look Kassidy in the eyes. "I know it hurts like hell right now, but you will be okay."

"I know." Kassidy gave a tiny, wry smile. "Thanks, Mom."

In a while, Hope had prepared a baked pasta dish put together with some ground beef she'd found in the freezer, a few cans of tomatoes and some other ingredients. She'd also found some buns, spread them with garlic butter and toasted them under the broiler.

It tasted pretty good, even though Chris hadn't felt hungry, and anyway he wouldn't be rude to Hope by not eating. Dag apparently felt the same, eating a big plateful and two buns. Kassidy ate a little.

Chris helped Hope clean up after. She insisted on doing the dishes, and he started the dishwasher while she wiped off the counter and cleaned the sink, leaving the kitchen spotless. Kassidy sat on the couch with Dag, Dave in a nearby armchair, watching the last period of the game. It wasn't the Blackhawks so nobody really cared about the game, but it was something, some noise to fill the room when nobody knew what to say.

Danielle arrived just as Kassidy's parents were leaving. Kassidy was hugged and sympathized with all over again. Danielle even cried too. And Kassidy got quieter.

Dag sensed Kassidy's distance when he climbed into bed that night. It wasn't overt. She wasn't pushing them away. She was drawing into herself though, and he felt it like a cold hand squeezing his guts. She slept between them as always, but on her stomach, face pressed to the pillow. He laid a hand on her ass, as he often did, sometimes even in his sleep, needing to be connected with her in some way.

"Babe," he murmured. "You okay?"

"Why does everyone keep asking me that?" She let out a sharp sigh. "I'm fine."

"You're not fine. You're hurting."

"Well, duh."

He closed his eyes. Shit.

She probably needed time. They all needed time.

Nobody'd asked how *he* was doing. Well, other than Chris. And when they'd asked each other that question, neither of them had told the truth. Chris wasn't one to talk about his feelings, and Dag felt like he shouldn't either. He needed to be strong so he could be there for Chris and Kass. Putting his emotions on them wouldn't help them.

They'd said they were okay. They weren't okay.

He wasn't okay, anyway. His insides felt frozen and empty. He was worried sick about Kassidy, concerned about Chris too, and struggling to make sense of it all through his view of it.

He, who'd never thought he'd be a father, had begun to look forward to this baby so much. Yeah, he was still terrified, but thinking about making a family had gradually pulled him in. He had hopes and dreams too for this baby, a boy or a girl who he knew would be smart and strong and have an incredible future. Envisioning that future for his child filled him with excitement and longing.

But no longer.

Crazy thoughts went through his head. Guilt. Worry about whether they'd ever be able to have another baby. Would Kassidy ever want to risk trying this again? Would any of them?

They'd been happy with the life they had before Kassidy got pregnant. Maybe a baby would have gotten in the way of things they'd wanted to do. His business. Chris's career. Kassidy's project and career. Going out and having fun without any encumbrances. They would go back to living like that and it would all be fine. Yeah.

7

Chris and Dag had tried to talk her out of going to work on Monday morning, telling her she could take a sick day and stay home and rest more. But Kassidy wanted to go to work. Lying around moping about things would make her crazy. At work, nobody knew. Nobody had to know.

She arrived in her cubicle and found a big cup of her favorite Starbucks coffee waiting for her. Thanks to Damon, who often did this. She couldn't drink the entire big cups of coffee he brought her, but still…it was thoughtful.

Today she could drink a grande coffee if she wanted. Maybe even two.

She picked it up and took a sip as she booted up her computer.

Focus on work.

Wow, the presentation they'd given Friday seemed a lifetime ago. She'd been so exhilarated by how it had gone, and when Chris had told her how impressed everyone had been, especially Daksh, the VP of Human Resources, who would make the decision about who would replace Kassidy's boss Paul when he retired next year. She'd been thrilled to hear their comments.

Now, that didn't seem to matter at all. No excitement sparked in her. She felt dead inside.

Just like the baby she'd been carrying.

She closed her eyes at the stab of pain then shut it down. She didn't want to feel that pain. She didn't want to feel anything.

"Morning." Damon spoke from the opening of her cubicle.

She sucked in a breath and opened her eyes to look at him, forcing a smile. "Good morning." She held up her cup. "Thanks for the coffee."

"You're welcome." His smile faded as he studied her. "You feeling okay, Kassidy?"

She opened her mouth to say, sure, yes, fine...but the words wouldn't come out. How could she tell him the truth though?

Her hand started shaking and she carefully set the cardboard cup on her desk. She placed her hands in her lap and curled her fingers together.

"No offense, but you don't look great," Damon said, a notch appearing between his eyebrows. "Do you need to go home?"

She shook her head. "No," she managed to say. She swallowed. "Maybe we should step into a meeting room."

His frown deepened but he stepped aside so she could precede him down the corridor. She closed the door and turned to face him. "I had a miscarriage over the weekend," she said quietly, looking at the carpet.

Silence.

"Oh man," Damon finally murmured. He moved closer and took her hands. Not appropriate. Touching between colleagues. But she didn't pull back. They were friends, kind of. And he was offering sympathy. "I had no idea."

"I know. We hadn't told many people."

"I'm so sorry, Kassidy. That sucks."

She nodded, tightening her lips to keep them from trembling. "It does suck. A lot."

"Are you okay?"

She resisted the urge to roll her eyes. God, if she heard that one more time she was going to punch someone. "Sure. I'm fine."

"No wonder you look so pale. You must have had a rough weekend."

She nodded and swallowed again.

He squeezed her hands and she lifted her head to meet his eyes. They were warm and full of sympathy, his mouth in a somber line. She sensed his desire to comfort her and was almost ready for him to pull her into his arms for a hug. Which would be *really* inappropriate. Instead, they stood looking at each other, holding hands.

"I'm sorry," he said again. "Don't even know what else to say."

"There is nothing else to say," she said quietly. She drew her hands away and stepped back. "So. Things went well Friday. Now we have more work to do."

He nodded, lips pursed, eyes shadowed. "Yeah," he said slowly. "We do."

Kassidy turned to leave the meeting room, their need for private conversation over. Through the glass window of the room she saw co-workers arriving to start their day. She caught the eye of Christy, taking off her coat in the corridor and watching her and Damon with her mouth hanging open.

Whatever.

"Good Morning, Christy," she said as she passed by the other woman to return to her cubicle. "How was your weekend?"

"Uh, great."

Kassidy gave her a curve of the lips. "Good."

Back at her desk, she rapidly consumed her coffee as she clicked through e-mails, followed up on tasks and prioritized her day. She had time to get a lot done before meetings that would take up the afternoon.

Focus on work.

Her mind didn't cooperate with that, however. She found herself flipping back and forth between tasks. She'd be reading over some of the training materials she'd gathered as research and suddenly need to check her e-mails. Then she noticed a broken nail and pulled an emery board out of her drawer to even it up. While she filed her nail, her mind wandered…remembering the pain of the cramps, the bleak despair…

Work. Focus on work.

Suddenly she felt so tired. Overwhelmingly, mind numbingly exhausted. She wasn't sure she could even drag her body out of her chair. She sat for a few minutes. Her eyes fell on the empty coffee cup.

Coffee. She'd get more coffee. That would get her through the day.

She managed to gather enough energy to rise, put on her coat and grab her purse. She rode the elevator down to the ground floor and exited the building onto Erie Street. In a distant part of her brain she registered the clear blue sky, the bright sun, the breeze that hinted at spring. Starbucks was across the street and she began to cross.

A blaring horn startled her, and she jumped back as a car, braking hard, skidded past her. Her hand flew to her throat and adrenaline shot through her veins, leaving her weak and shaky. The driver of the car turned and flipped her the bird.

Holy shit. That was close. Where had that car come from?

She hadn't even looked. God. She was a walking menace. She carefully checked for traffic before walking across the street.

She stood in line in Starbucks, studying the pastries, heart still thudding, knees still wobbly. The person behind her nudged her, startling her again. The man lifted his chin at the barista ready to take her order.

"Oh," she said. "Sorry. Um, I'll have a...a grande..." She blinked. She had no idea what she wanted. "Grande café latte."

She fumbled in her purse to pay for it then waited for her drink to be prepared. She needed to get it together.

She managed to accomplish...well, not very much, by lunch time. Often she brought a lunch and ate in the break room with some of her co-worker friends. Today she hadn't made a lunch and she wasn't hungry anyway, so she kept working. Or trying to work. Then it was one o'clock and time for a meeting with her team.

She dug deep for the strength to lead the meeting but halfway through the hour session was horrified to find herself stopping mid-sentence because she had no idea what she was supposed to say. She blinked and looked down at her file. Still nothing.

"Sorry," she murmured to her gang. "I'm, uh..."

Alarmingly, tears came into her eyes. Christ! She could not cry in front of everyone.

"Excuse me." She rose and rushed from the room before they could see her wet eyes.

In the ladies' room, she locked herself into a stall, sat on the toilet and tried to compose herself, but it was a lost cause. The tears refused to stop.

What the hell? She'd thought she was done with the crying. She tried not to sob out loud, swallowing hard, breathing shaky breaths in and out. She dabbed at her eyes with toilet paper, blew her nose. She'd look like a wreck when she finally emerged.

Maybe she should have stayed home. This was stupid.

She'd been gone so long that Lissa came looking for her. The bathroom door opened and Lissa's voice called softly, "Kassidy? Are you in here?"

Shit. Kassidy dropped her head. "Yes," she said.

"Are you okay?"

There was that fucking annoying question again. "I'm not feeling so well."

"Can I do anything?"

"No. I-I might just go home."

"Want me to get Chris?"

Yes. She wanted Chris. She wanted Chris and Dag to come rescue her and make everything okay. They were her heroes, the men she loved, but even they couldn't make this okay. They would only get more worried and overprotective. "No," she choked out. "I don't want to bother him."

"I'll wait for you," Lissa said.

"No, that's okay. If you could you get my coat and my purse? Purse is in my bottom left drawer."

"Sure."

The door opened and closed with a soft thud. Kassidy left the stall and faced herself in the mirror. Oh yeah, a mess. Smeared mascara, red eyes, pink nose. Lovely. She tried to repair some of the damage and faced Lissa when she came back.

"Want me to go with you?" Lissa asked, concern tightening her pretty face. "I don't know if you should go home alone."

"I'm okay." Kassidy forced a tight smile. "I'll see you tomorrow. Can you tell the others we'll reschedule the meeting? And also tell Damon I've gone home and I won't be at our other meetings later."

"Sure. I can do that."

Kassidy just wanted out of there before anyone saw her crying, so she hurried down the corridor, head down.

Out on the street, she took a long breath. She couldn't stay at work, but the idea of going home and being there alone in her misery made her skin crawl. She began to walk, no idea where she was going.

She felt some vague cramps in her abdomen, once again

reminding her of her loss. Exhaustion swept over her. Probably she should be home resting, but she couldn't bear that idea.

She went into a restaurant, a small diner, ordered a sandwich and another coffee. She took two bites of the sandwich, but drank the coffee. She sat for a while, gazing out the window at passing traffic and pedestrians. The waitress refilled her coffee, and she drank that one too. Well. She couldn't sit there all day.

After leaving the diner, she walked to Michigan Avenue. There was Bloomingdales. She'd go shopping. Just not for baby things.

She passed through the cosmetic department, breathing in the scents of exotic perfumes, wandered through the shoe department and then into clothing racks. Shopping for shoes and clothes was something she usually enjoyed. She studied a pretty blouse with no enthusiasm whatsoever. It didn't matter. Nothing mattered.

Her cell phone buzzed in her purse. She paused to check it. Chris. Holy crap. It was five-thirty. She answered. "Hi."

"Kass, where are you? I came down to your office to get you to go home and they said you left hours ago. Are you okay?"

Fuck. There was that urge to punch something again. "Yes, I'm okay. I'm shopping."

Not really, but whatever.

"Shopping? They said you went home sick."

"Oh. Yeah. I did. I wasn't really sick. I just had to leave."

"Shit, Kass. Where are you? I'll come get you."

"No. That's okay." She picked up a cashmere sweater in a pretty shade of blue. "I'm going to look around a bit more. I'll see you later."

She heard his frustrated noise as she said, "Bye," and ended the call.

Guilt over being so cavalier pricked her conscience. He was probably worried about her.

Everyone was worried about her. It weighed on her, heavy, like she was being smothered. She just wanted to be alone.

Her phone kept buzzing but she kept ignoring it. She tried on a pair of jeans, but glumly regarded herself in the mirror. She'd put on a few pounds. It looked fine when she was pregnant. Now she wasn't pregnant. Now she looked fat. She left the jeans in the change room.

After she left Bloomingdales she passed a pub. Hey, she could drink. There was an idea. She entered the small, dark bar and found a stool at the bar. She ordered a glass of white wine and watched a news show on the TV above the bar. Midway through her second glass of wine she started to feel pretty buzzed. Not only had she not eaten much all day, she hadn't had alcohol for over two months. Two glasses would be it.

But then she'd have to leave.

She still didn't want to go home.

She was being stupid. She had to go home. Dag and Chris were probably freaking out.

On the train, she checked her phone. Eight missed calls. Three voicemails. Ten text messages. Wow.

More squeezing weight pressing in on her from all sides. Jesus, couldn't people just leave her alone for a while?

Maybe she was too selfish to be a mom. Maybe that was why this had happened. She stared out the dark window.

When she got home and walked in the front door, she blinked at seeing Sarah in their living room. "Oh. Hi."

Dag and Chris, of course, both leaped up from where they sat on the couch and rushed at her. The force of their concern came at her like a brick wall, and she held up her hands, panic buzzing inside her. "I'm okay," she said. "Whoa."

"Jesus, Kass," Chris muttered. "What the hell?"

They both stopped without touching her. Her chest started to hurt. She looked at Sarah.

"I came to see you," Sarah said quietly. "I was about to give up and go home."

"Sorry," Kassidy said, shrugging off her coat as she walked in. "I didn't know you were here."

"You would if you answered your fucking phone," Chris growled.

She cast him a narrow-eyed look. "I needed some space," she said. She looked back at Sarah. "Where are Jeff and Jaden?"

"At home. Hopefully Jaden's in bed. I asked Jeff if he wanted to come and he said no." She made a face. "Not that he doesn't want to see you. He's all uncomfortable and doesn't know what to say."

Kassidy smiled a crooked smile. "Hey, I get it." She sat on the end of the couch near the chair Sarah sat in. "Thanks for coming."

"I wanted to apologize."

Whoa. There was something different than the usual *Are you okay?* "What for?"

"The night you told us you were pregnant." Sarah looked down, then up again. "I was a bitch."

Kassidy studied her friend's face. "Yeah. You kind of were." She might not have been that honest with her friend before. Now, it didn't seem to matter. "No, not a bitch. But you did kind of tick me off. Why?"

"I honestly don't know." Sarah met her eyes. "I was happy for you, Kass. I really was. I didn't mean to be all negative. I guess sometimes I get frustrated and tired. It *is* hard being a mom. But now..." Her eyes went glossy. "I feel horrible. I had some weird idea I was helping you see the reality of motherhood. But you didn't need that. All you needed was for me to say, congratulations, you'll be a great mom." She leaned forward. "And you will be. Some day. And now all you need for me to say is, I'm sorry and I'm here for you."

"Thank you, Sarah." Kassidy's throat ached.

Sarah reached out and grabbed one of Kassidy's hands. "Take your time getting over this. It has to be hard. And we're *all* here for you. I wanted you to know that."

Kassidy nodded. "I know. I just...I don't know what I need right now. I'm all messed up."

Aware of the guys listening, her stomach tightened. The words were meant for them too.

She was messed up. For the first time since she and Chris and Dag had come together as three, she felt like it was too much. Their presence and overpowering concern and care for her felt oppressive and smothering. It was too much.

And that filled her with even more despair.

8

"Are you fucking kidding me?" Chris rubbed the back of his neck and stared at Dag, standing in their bedroom.

Dag looked lost. A hard shudder worked through Chris. Dag never looked lost. He always gave the appearance of being confident and carefree. Tonight, there was no mask and Dag's raw pain was evident.

"She wants to sleep alone," Dag said with a bewildered crease on his forehead, repeating what Kassidy had just told them.

Chris sighed. "I guess we need to give her 'space'. That's what she said she needs."

"She doesn't need fucking space," Dag growled. "She needs *us*."

Chris's forehead tightened. "I agree," he said quietly. "But she doesn't. And I'm kinda worried about that."

"Yeah. Me too. Fuck."

Kassidy was sleeping in the guest room.

"You think she blames us for this?" Chris asked.

Dag's eyebrows slanted down. "Christ. I don't know. But that's ridiculous. This isn't our fault."

Chris nodded, even though guilt still jabbed at him. "It wasn't anything we did that caused the miscarriage."

"I know. But one of us got her knocked up, and that's what led to all this."

"Yeah." Chris reached behind his head and pulled his T-shirt off. "But I don't think she's blaming us. If anything, she's blaming herself."

"Fuck."

"I know." Chris stepped out of his jeans and tossed them over the arm of a chair. His underwear followed. "We'll give her space, let her have some alone time tonight. I don't like it, but hell, I don't know what else to do."

Dag nodded. "I guess we don't know what she's going through. This is so shitty."

"Yeah." Chris slid into bed. The sheets felt cold against his skin. He needed company. "Get in here."

Dag's lips lifted in a small smile. "Be right there."

Now also naked, he strode to the bathroom. Chris clicked off the light then flopped onto his belly, face buried in the pillow. A few minutes later Dag climbed into bed with him.

"Feels weird without Kassidy here," Dag said.

"Yeah." It sure the hell did.

Dag pushed over closer. The heat of his body warmed Chris and he closed his eyes as Dag laid his head on his back. Dag's hand stroked over his lower back, then his ass and hip. "Glad we've got each other though."

Chris gave a mute nod. It was true. They had each other. Thank fuck.

Dag's big hand rubbing over him started to warm him. Started to make his groin buzz. Shit. Was it okay to get turned on at a time like this?

He slowly rolled to his back. Dag lay on his side next to him, and his hand now moved over Chris's hip and his abs. Dag shifted and bent his head, his tongue dragging over Chris's tight abs, his mouth opening in a long, slow kiss. He licked up higher, nipped at Chris's nipple with his lips, sending a jolt of heat to Chris's dick, then kissed his collarbone, his shoulder, the side of his neck.

"Fuck, man," Chris sighed, unwillingly aroused.

"Need you," Dag murmured near his ear. "Really, really need you right now, Chris."

"Yeah. Me too."

Dag started licking and kissing his way back down Chris's torso, slowly, sensually, lovingly. Chris's abs tightened as Dag licked over his lower belly, then, oh yeah, Dag's hand closed around Chris's cock and lifted it to his mouth. Dag licked over the head, swirled his tongue around it, took it inside his mouth in slow, short sucking pulls. Chris lifted his arms and folded them behind his head on the pillow, eyes closed. Sensation poured through him in slow, hot waves.

"Feels good," he moaned in a low voice. "So damn good."

Dag kept licking and sucking, his fist tight at the base of Chris's cock, sliding up and down in slow, sure strokes. Chris's balls tightened and the buzzing intensified. But Dag released him and pushed up.

Chris opened heavy eyes to watch as Dag moved over him, straddling him. His throat tightened a little, love expanding in his chest as he took in Dag's shadowy shape, his wide shoulders, lean waist, dark hair and eyes. Dag positioned himself over Chris's hips and fisted their cocks together in one hand. Chris's eyes lowered there to watch. Fuck, that was hot.

Dag stroked their cocks together then lifted his chin. "Lube," he murmured.

Chris pulled his arm out from behind his head and awkwardly managed to get the drawer open on his side of the bed. He groped around and pulled the bottle of lube out by feel alone. He tossed it at Dag. With a flash of white teeth in the dim room, Dag caught it. Soon they were both slicked up, Dag's hands sliding over their cocks pressed together.

Again, Chris watched. So fucking hot. So fucking beautiful. Heat rushed through his body and his skin prickled all over.

Dag let go then and leaned forward to kiss him. Dag's mouth was hot and hard on his, his tongue strong and insistent as he pushed into Chris's mouth. Yeah. Oh yeah. He needed this so much.

Dag pushed back up, his cock thick and hard on Chris's lower belly, and reached behind himself for Chris's shaft. Finding it, he rose up on his knees. Eyes fastened on Chris's, Dag found his own anus, rubbing the lubed-up head over it. His jaw tightened and then he lowered himself onto Chris, sucking in a sharp breath.

"Fuck yeah," Chris groaned. Pleasure slammed through him as Dag's body closed around him, so fucking tight and hot.

Dag lowered himself more, slowly, taking him all the way, his eyelids dropping almost closed over his eyes as he did so. "Chris," he muttered. "Damn. Love your dick in my ass."

"Yeah."

Dag moved slowly, his eyes open but still heavy-lidded, meeting Chris's. He rose and fell, and the pull and drag of Dag's body on his cock had electricity sparking and building at the base of his spine. Chris extended a hand up and laid it on Dag's chest, rubbing over his pecs, flicking his nipples, making him gasp and twitch.

Then Dag got his feet beneath him, planted firmly into the mattress beside Chris's hips in a crouch, and he leaned back, arms straight out behind him, propping himself up. Chris's gaze dropped to Dag's cock, enormous and thrusting out aggressively, bouncing as they moved together. He reached for it, unable to resist touching him, unable to resist having that thick, pulsing rod in his hand. Chris's other hand landed on Dag's big knee and gripped it. He watched his hand jerking Dag with slow, insistent strokes, then looked up at Dag, watching him back, his lips parted, eyes glittering in the dim room.

"Fuck me," Dag murmured. "Just like that."

"Yeah." Chris's hips lifted, thrusting up into Dag, still slow but harder, Dag's body rocking back against him. They fucked each other with slow, forceful impacts.

The tension in Chris's spine rose painfully, his breathing growing harsh. His balls tightened even more at the base of his cock. He loved this. He loved Dag. This all seemed right in a world that had gone so wrong.

Dag pushed up again, bent over Chris, now planting his fists into the mattress above Chris's head, arms straight. His face hung close to Chris's, his body curved over his, their hips still moving, fucking, their eyes joined in intense, intimate contact. Dag's mouth brushed his, once, again, then kissed him hard. Chris hands went to Dag's thighs.

They fucked like that for long, measured moments, Chris's cock sliding in and out of Dag's body in slow, sensuous glides punctuated with hot, hard kisses. Pleasure licked up over every nerve ending like flames. His breath wrenched in and out of him. "Fuck me," he groaned. "Gonna come. Now…"

"Yeah. Do it. Now. Fucking now…"

Chris reached for his own cock, gripping the base as pressure built and then pleasure exploded through his nerves, a searing line of electricity from his balls out his cock. Dag lifted off him and Chris came, spurting onto Dag's ass in hot, powerful pulses. He grunted and groaned his way through his climax hard, wrenching pulses.

"Yeah," Dag groaned. "Hell yeah. Now me…so close…" He whipped his leg over Chris's hips and knee-walked up the bed so he was right beside Chris's head. Holding his cock with one hand, his other hand slid beneath Chris's neck, lifting his head, and he pulled Chris's mouth to the head of his cock. Chris opened hungrily, eager to take him in, his body still buzzing, but

Dag was coming already. Dag rubbed his dick over Chris's mouth, and Chris groaned as Dag's hot semen landed on his lips and tongue and chin.

Dag held his cock, his hand slowing on it, his fingers relaxing on the back of Chris's neck, then he lowered Chris's head to the pillow.

"Fuck, I love you," Dag mumbled with one last, long squeezing pull on his dick. He fell to the bed and stretched out next to Chris, throwing an arm and a leg over him.

Chris wrapped his own arm around Dag's and held on tight. "Me too. Love you too. We're gonna get through this."

"Yeah. We have to." Dag's mouth sought out his for a long kiss. "We have to."

Kassidy slept apart from them the next night too. Chris and Dag got into bed together, again alone, and again it felt all wrong. Dag lay on his back staring into the darkness.

"What if she never wants to try again?" Chris said from beside him. Kassidy had been to the doctor that day, who'd told her she was fine and there should be no reason she couldn't get pregnant again. She hadn't seemed all that happy about the news.

Dag didn't answer right away. He'd been thinking about that too. "Maybe that would be better," he said slowly. "We had things great before this. All the freedom in the world, time to do the things we want to do. Travel. Not worry about babysitters and diapers and feeding schedules."

Chris's head turned on the pillow next to him. Dag felt his eyes on him. "Are you serious?"

"Sure." His body tightened. "Not to mention, we wouldn't have to go through this again."

Chris's head moved on the pillow. "You don't want to try again?"

"Do you?" Dag still stared straight up at the ceiling. "Why would we put ourselves through that again?" He sighed, then rolled and reached for Chris. Chris's body was solid and he resisted Dag's attempt to pull him in. "What? What's wrong?"

"What's wrong? Are you seriously asking that?"

"Shit. I know what's wrong. I mean, with you. Talk to me."

Chris's muscles tightened even more beneath his hand. "What's to talk about? It happened. We need to deal with it and move on."

Dag processed that. There was nothing at all wrong with what Chris had just said. That was what he wanted too. Deal with it. Move on.

But it felt wrong. He rolled to his back again and sighed. He just wanted things back the way they were before the miscarriage. Maybe this would just take time.

Last night, he and Chris had come together, helping each other deal with the pain, loving each other. Tonight, he felt a wall between them. Not only did Kassidy sleep apart from them, they slept apart from each other, even though they were in the same bed. And that made a tight fear crawl up Dag's spine.

For the next week, Kassidy slept in the other room. She went to work every day. She said she was okay. She wasn't eating a lot. Dag watched her with eagle-eyed scrutiny. She worked late a lot. This for some reason really annoyed Chris.

He and Chris argued about what to do about it. There was an undercurrent of tension now between them, something dark and disturbing. Chris wanted to storm into the guest room and haul her out of there. Dag reminded him she was fragile and hurting and they should back off and let her heal. He hated it, but he didn't know what else to do for her. He didn't know how to help her other than do what she asked.

She talked to them. She acted like things were normal, but despite her stiff smiles, her eyes were sad and when she thought nobody was watching her mouth drooped.

Dag's trip to Australia was coming up. He was supposed to leave this weekend. If he'd thought it was going to be difficult to leave before, when Kassidy had been pregnant, that was nothing compared to how hard it was now. With this uneasy discomfort now between him and Chris, and with Kassidy pulling away and distancing herself from both of them, he felt if he left, he risked losing everything.

Fuck. That could not happen.

He was at a loss as to what to do.

He'd never wanted to go on this trip. Yeah, he was excited about the contract. The money. The opportunity. The challenge. He loved all that.

He didn't love leaving his family behind at a time when things were so fucked up.

Late Friday afternoon, Kassidy was surprised when Damon said, "Let's knock off early for once."

She gave him wide eyes. "What? Got a hot date tonight or something?"

He laughed. "Nah. Let's go for a drink. It's Friday. We've been working hard. Things are going well and we're on target."

She considered that. "Okay." Why not? She'd been at the office late every night that week. They were busy, sure, but she was fully aware that part of the reason she worked late was because she didn't want to go home.

She knew she was letting down Dag and Chris. She'd

let them down in the worst possible way by losing the baby. On top of that, Dag was leaving tomorrow. Now there was no reason for him not to go to Australia, but it still made her angry every time she thought about it, which was unreasonable and stupid. How could she be angry at him?

She'd had a couple more episodes where she'd suddenly found herself in tears for no reason, fortunately not in the middle of a team meeting again. Since nobody else had known she was pregnant, they didn't realize what she was going through. This left her with an isolated, lonely feeling.

The only one who knew was Damon. He'd been amazingly understanding. She didn't want to talk about the miscarriage or the baby, or how her relationship seemed to be disintegrating because of this, but when she'd burst into tears, he'd calmly handed her a box of tissues and led her to an office and closed the door so they had privacy. He'd made sure she was okay, brought her coffee and handed her a bottle of Visine when she was done crying. He never pushed her to talk, but she had the feeling he'd listen if she wanted to. He treated her like he always had. He didn't make her feel scared and smothered.

They left the office and walked to Brix Wine Bar, not far away. With dark walls and floor and furnishings, carefully lit with both spots of halogen lights and chandeliers dripping with crystals, the bar had a classy but cozy feel, buzzing with Friday happy hour energy. Voices and clinking glasses filled the air along with strains of jazz music.

They sat at a small, high table for two on stools and took a few moments to peruse the extensive selection of wines by the glass.

"Are you a red wine or a white wine drinker?" Damon asked.

"I like both. Right now I feel like red. Something rich."

He grinned. "If that means expensive, we've come to the right place."

She made a face. "I didn't mean expensive. I meant rich tasting."

The waiter who'd appeared heard their comments. "If I can make a suggestion," he said. "For something big and ripe, the Rancho Vignola Zinfandel is excellent."

"Sure," Kassidy said, closing her menu.

"I'll have the same," Damon said.

The waiter returned moments later with a small bowl of olives. Kassidy picked one up and popped it in her mouth. "I love olives."

"Me too." Damon reached for one as well. "This is a nice place." He looked around.

"I've been here a couple of times. It's close to the office, so it's good for after work drinks. Busy tonight."

"It's Friday. It's the weekend. We should make a point of doing this every Friday after a long week."

She tried to smile in agreement. Her mouth felt stiff.

They talked a little shop, then the conversation moved on to some of the people working on the team. "Daksh was asking me for feedback about your work the other day," he said. "Maybe I shouldn't be telling you this." Then he shrugged. "It was just informal."

"Did you tell him I've been screwing up all week, forgetting things and bursting into tears at inappropriate times?"

Damon smiled. "No. I didn't tell him that. Everything I said was positive."

"Thanks."

"Kassidy, you're going through a hard time right now. You'll get through this. Of course I didn't tell him those things."

"I appreciate how understanding you've been this week. That was so unprofessional to start crying like that.

I'm embarrassed." She made a face. "The doctor said hormones could still be influencing my mood, and that trouble concentrating is understandable."

"Of course it is," Damon said quietly. "You've been through a tragedy. You could have taken time off, you know."

"I know. I didn't want to. I thought I'd be better off distracting myself with work. I didn't realize it would be so hard though."

"You're doing fine. Although you look like you've lost weight."

"Really?" Kassidy looked down at herself. "I'd put on weight when I was pregnant."

"Phhht. Not much, if any. And if you did, you've lost it."

She made a face. "I haven't had much appetite this week."

"That's no good. You have to eat."

"Don't start lecturing me. I get enough of that at home."

"Sorry." His smile went crooked. "It'll take time for you to get through this. Not that I have any experience."

"I didn't expect…" She stopped. "I didn't expect it to cause so much…I don't know. I shouldn't even be talking to you about this."

"You haven't been going home from work with Chris this week. Are things okay with you two?"

His quiet question didn't seem intrusive. He sounded concerned.

"It's kind of hard to explain," she said.

The waiter arrived with their glasses of wine, generous pours in big, lovely glasses. Kassidy picked hers up to taste it. "Mmm, very nice. It is big and ripe."

Damon tasted his as well and nodded. "Great. A new favorite."

"Are you into wine?"

"Not seriously. An old girlfriend made me take wine tasting classes with her. It was kind of interesting."

"Wine tasting classes. That would be fun." Something Dag might do with her. Her stomach clenched thinking about Dag.

"The problem's not with Chris," she said, needing him to know that. "It's with me."

"How so?"

"I'm so messed up inside. At first I was hurting. So sad. Then, I didn't feel anything. I was numb. I didn't *want* to feel anything. Then I started feeling…smothered. Like everybody was worried about me."

"I'm sure they were."

"They don't need to be. I'm fine."

"You mean physically fine or emotionally fine?"

She blinked. "Um. Physically. I lost the baby, but I survived. I'm okay."

"Emotionally?"

She sighed. "I'm a wreck. I don't even know what I feel anymore."

"Have you talked to Chris about it?"

She bit her bottom lip. "Not really."

"That's probably something you should do."

She nodded slowly then sipped her wine. "Yes. I guess…" She let out a sigh. Things were so much more complicated than Damon knew. It wasn't only Chris. There were three of them in this mess. "I'm afraid I'll screw things up even more. How do I tell him I feel like he's smothering me?" And how did she tell Dag she felt like he was abandoning her?

"You're a good communicator, Kassidy. You'll find a way."

She gave him a crooked smile. "Thanks."

The waiter approached to see if they wanted another glass of wine. They both agreed to another of the same, and Damon said, "Maybe we should have something to eat. So we don't get schnockered."

Kassidy gave a choked a laugh. "Might be a good idea."

They ordered a few things from the small plates menu to share—crab cakes, a duck paté with toast points, and rosemary parmesan fries.

When the waiter had left again, Damon said, "You and Chris aren't married, are you?"

"No." Again, how could she explain things to him? She considered herself married, even if not legally. To both Chris and Dag. They were in a long-term, committed relationship, and the lack of legal documentation had never been an issue for them. They'd made promises to each other that they all considered sacred and binding.

She looked down at the ring on the third finger of her left hand, the wide swirl of gold around the big diamond sparkling in the light hanging above the table. She loved her ring.

Tears came to her eyes again. "Shit," she muttered, swiping at them just as the waiter replaced their empty glasses with full ones.

"Sorry. Didn't mean to upset you." His forehead wrinkled with concern. "Are things that bad between you?"

"I don't know. Oh shit. I'm sorry."

"Look, I don't work for RBM. If you want to talk to me, go ahead. It won't impact your career at all. You know I already think highly of you professionally. And..." He stopped. "That won't change."

She eyed him. For some reason, she longed to spill out everything that was inside her. "It's not just Chris," she blurted out. "It's Dag."

Damon blinked.

"We live in a polyamorous relationship," she continued. "All three of us. Chris, Dag and me. We wanted this baby. Chris and Dag were both the fathers of it. So it's a little more complicated than just Chris and me."

"Uh, yeah. Okay." He gave his head a small shake. "I have to say I didn't expect to hear that."

She bit her lip. "Some people don't get it, so we don't

tell everyone. Friends and family know, of course. You won't say anything to anyone at RBM, will you?"

"No, of course not. I...well." He looked at her with an expression she couldn't read. "You love both of them?"

"Yes." She held his gaze.

He nodded, and she thought she saw disappointment before he lowered his eyes. Her insides tightened. Maybe she shouldn't be having this conversation with Damon. There'd been little things she'd picked up on as they worked together. She knew he liked her. Was he hoping for more from her? Yet he knew she was in a committed relationship with Chris.

A relationship that was struggling.

"I do love them both," she repeated firmly. Fiercely. Determinedly.

The waiter arrived with the food they'd ordered. Kassidy hadn't eaten much all week and was already feeling the slight wooziness from one big glass of wine. But although the food had sounded good when they ordered it, now she looked at it with distaste.

"Eat," Damon said firmly. "Take a few bites. You'll be surprised how easy it will go down."

She picked up a French fry, golden hot and seasoned with rosemary and parmesan cheese. It *was* really good. She had another one, then spread a little pâté onto a toast point and ate that too. "It is good," she agreed.

For a few moments they focused on the food and wine. Then Kassidy said, "Maybe we shouldn't be doing this."

He didn't ask what she meant. He looked at his wine glass, took a gulp, then said, "It's okay, Kassidy. I get it. I just want to be here for you. A friend. We're co-workers, for now, but that's temporary, and like I said, I don't work for RBM. If you want to talk about things, I'm here to listen. I hate seeing you so unhappy."

Her chest ached a little more, but she nodded. "Thanks."

"So. Talk to me."

She told him how happy they'd all been about the baby. The hopes and dreams they'd shared for their child. How hard it had been to lose that. "Some of our friends said to try again. I don't know if I can do that. It feels like that would dishonor Belly Bean."

He blinked.

She huffed out a laugh and waved a hand. "That was our name for the baby. It doesn't feel right to just try again right away. He or she was important."

Damon nodded.

"And I'm terrified it'll happen again. Um, are you sure you want to hear all this? I'm a mess."

"It's okay."

"I was worried about my career," she now said, not sure where all this stuff was coming from. "When I got pregnant. I started thinking about work and I felt guilty about leaving before the project was done." She winced. "How could I have been worried about my career and put that ahead of the baby? I would've been a terrible mother."

"Kassidy." Damon shook his head. "God, no."

"And then when it happened, everybody kept asking me if I was okay. Chris and Dag were treating me like I was glass, being so careful and trying to look after me, and I felt like they were smothering me. I couldn't stand it." She closed her eyes briefly, searching for words. "I guess what I really felt was...guilty. Like I didn't deserve their care."

"Why would you feel that way?" Damon asked quietly.

She forced herself to say the words. "I feel like a failure as a woman. I'm the woman in this triad. I'm the one who can give them a baby. And I couldn't even do that." She took a sip of wine to ease the tightness of her throat. "I let them down," she whispered. "I let them down in the worst way. And I don't know how to ever make it up to them."

Damon looked startled. "Oh, Kassidy." He reached a

hand across the small table and laid his on top of hers, leaning closer. "That's not right."

"It's the truth." She pressed her lips together. "Tomorrow, Dag is leaving for Australia for six months. On business."

She wasn't sure why she'd spilled that detail.

"You sound angry about that."

Her stomach twisted. "We thought he was going to miss most of my pregnancy," she said slowly. "I was a little upset about that. But now, it doesn't matter."

"No?"

His warm eyes watched her. She took in a long, slow breath. It did matter. Of course it mattered. She *was* angry. Did this all mean nothing to him that he could just leave? How could he leave them now?

She was silent for a moment. Then the words rose to her lips and she uttered the thought that scared her the most. "I've wondered if they'd be better off without me." She'd heard them, that first night she'd slept alone, making love without her. They didn't need her.

Damon said nothing. The air around them went very still and the noise in the bar faded into a mute blur. The words hung there between them.

She shouldn't have been dumping this crap on him. He'd offered, but still. She could see he had no idea what to say or do. But just saying the words, getting them out there, made her face them. Her heart rose into her throat, nearly choking her, her insides clumped into a painful snarl.

Finally Damon said, "I don't know you all very well. I know you, I know Chris a little, I don't know your other… I don't know Dag at all. But I don't believe that can possibly be true, Kassidy."

She nodded miserably. It was easy for Damon to say that, but it was true, he didn't know them at all.

"Look," Damon continued. "You've probably caught on

to the fact that I'm attracted to you. If I thought there was any chance that your relationship with those two guys was over, I'd be putting hard moves on you. But you already told me you love them. Both of them. I know Chris loves you. That's pretty clear when you're together. Hell, he worships you. I can't speak for Dag obviously, and I get that your relationship has to be complicated. On top of dealing with a miscarriage, you all are probably dealing with a mess of other things going on. Conflict between two people is hard; between three it's gotta be even worse."

She nodded again. He was not wrong about that. And he was also not wrong about the fact that she loved Chris and Dag and there was not going to be anything between Damon and her. His interest in her was flattering, but for her it was just a friendship between two people who worked together and got along well.

"But even though I don't know all of you that well, I can't believe they would be better off without you." He shook his head.

She swallowed. "Thank you."

"Don't worry," Damon said wryly. "Monday morning, this conversation will never have happened. I have the utmost professional respect for you, Kassidy. This won't change anything."

"I hope not," she said honestly. "Because I really do enjoy working with you, and I'm really committed to this project."

"I know. And thanks."

"You're a great guy, Damon."

Their eyes met and he smiled at her. "Thanks."

She glanced at her watch. "Holy shit. I didn't realize what time it is." She sighed. "I should get home." Dag was leaving in the morning and despite her anger at him, she did feel guilty about not being there.

She'd told Damon her biggest fear. She'd said the words. Now she had to go home and face it.

9

At five o'clock on Friday, Chris called Kassidy see if she was coming home with him. As he'd done every night that week. And every night that week she'd said no. He got her voicemail and hung up. He tried her cell phone. Also voicemail. Jesus Christ.

He strode to the elevator and rode it down to the eighth floor, made his way through cubeland to her cubicle. She wasn't there. He frowned. He poked his head into Lissa's cubicle. "Hey, Lissa. You know where Kassidy is?"

Lissa looked at him with wide eyes and then blinked rapidly. "Um. She's already gone for the day. She and Damon left a little while ago."

Chris kept his face neutral, but his gut did a hard leap. "Oh. Okay, thanks." He forced a casual smile and turned toward the elevator.

What. The. Fuck. She'd left with Damon fucking Orr?

His eyes narrowed as he grabbed his cell phone and called her again. Still no answer. As usual, lately. Fuck this shit.

He went back to his own office and threw himself into the chair behind his desk, staring out the window, not even seeing the downtown Chicago skyline there.

His admin assistant Wendy appeared in his door. "I'm

off now," she said. "Have a—" Then she frowned. "You okay?"

He looked at her blankly.

She took another step into the room. "Chris? What's wrong?"

He shook his head. "Nothing. Just went to get Kassidy to go home and she's already left."

"Uh..." Wendy shifted and twisted her fingers together. "You know she left with Damon Orr." It wasn't a question.

He again strove not to show his anger and frustration. "Yeah."

Wendy said nothing. Her eyes darted all over the room. "Okay, I'm just going to say it," she finally said. "There are rumors going around about Kassidy and Damon."

He snapped upright in his chair. "What?"

She held up a hand. "First of all, don't shoot the messenger. Second, I know they're not true. You know what the grapevine is like in this place. But this is what people are saying. There've been a lots of closed door meetings between those two. Lots of late nights when they've been alone in the office."

That was true. Chris said nothing.

"Christy saw them holding hands. She swears it's true. In one of the meeting rooms with windows, they were holding hands and staring into each other's eyes." She winced. "Not sure how to explain that one. But I know it doesn't mean anything."

His eyes bugged out. He couldn't help it. He struggled for control.

"Then today, they left early together. It added fuel to the rumor fire."

Heat rose from beneath his dress shirt, washing up into his face. He wanted to punch someone. Something. Toss his computer through the plate glass window. His back teeth ground together.

"I thought you should know," Wendy said. "I told

everyone they're crazy. You two are solid. Kassidy would never do that. Damon…well, we don't know him, and damn, he's a hot guy."

Chris winced.

"Uh, sorry. But it's true and there are a lot of women here who'd kill to be having 'closed door meetings' with Damon Orr." She made the air quotes with her fingers. "That's probably why the rumors started. People are just jealous and small-minded."

Chris drew in a long breath, fighting for control. "Thanks, Wendy. Appreciate you letting me know."

Ever since she'd gotten married and Chris had given in and allowed her to take her honeymoon despite a looming project deadline and rules against vacation time then, Wendy had been unswervingly loyal and hardworking for him. Come to think of it, Kassidy had been the one who'd convinced him he had to let Wendy have that vacation time. Kassidy had known the consequences, and if he'd said no, Wendy probably would have quit and he wouldn't have had such a great assistant the last few years.

"Go home," he said. "Have a good weekend."

"Thanks. You too."

Though she looked like she doubted *that* was going to happen.

He doubted it too.

With no idea where Kassidy and Damon had gone or if they were coming back, and her not answering calls or texts, he left his office and descended all the way to the underground parking where his car was.

He had to resist the urge to stomp on the gas pedal and squeal out of the parking garage. His jaw tight, he pulled out onto the street and into traffic. Rush hour. Slow. Stupid drivers doing stupid things. It made his head pound and his jaw ache.

Maybe he was overreacting. Maybe Kassidy was already home, waiting for him.

He knew that wasn't likely, after the week they'd had.

Dag, however, was home when he got there. "No Kassidy again?" he asked from the kitchen where he was opening a beer.

"Nope." Chris debated sharing what he'd just learned with Dag, then decided against it. He didn't need to get Dag upset about something that was probably nothing.

"Christ," Dag muttered. "I'm leaving tomorrow and she's not even here."

Chris sighed. He didn't even know what to say about that. Yeah, Dag was leaving. He was still pissed at Dag about his comments that they were better off without the baby. Now he was afraid Kassidy was falling for some other guy. Fuck. Let him leave. Leave Chris to deal with this shit.

His belly muscles rigid, mind churning, he trudged upstairs to change out of his suit and tie, a hard pulse in the pit of his stomach. He hoped to Christ what he'd heard was nothing. But Kassidy had been acting weird all week. Yeah, she was grieving, he got that, but why was she separating herself from them like that? Was there something to the rumors? She *had* been working late a lot with Damon, and that had been going on even before the miscarriage.

He hadn't felt this alone in…well, the last time he'd felt this way was three years ago when he and Dag had argued over Dag touching him sexually in bed and he'd kicked Dag out of their apartment, and then Kassidy had told him she was falling in love with Dag. He'd been terrified that he'd lost both of them.

He was feeling that way now. They were slipping away from him, somehow, and he didn't know what to do to get things back. He sat on the side of the bed, pressure building inside him, a dark, crushing feeling.

Last time Kassidy had kicked his ass and told him he had to go talk to Dag. She'd wanted them to figure things out between them and had pushed him to do that even though she'd been afraid that figuring things out between them might mean she was left out.

His chest ached and he let his head fall back, eyes closed. He wasn't sure if he'd ever appreciated the magnitude of what she'd done, the potential sacrifice she'd made. Because she loved him. She loved both of them, enough to step aside if that had been what they'd needed.

Was he supposed to do the same? Step aside so she could be with some other guy?

Fuck that bullshit.

Rage rose inside him, a hot surge, right up into his throat. Rage against Damon Orr. Was it wrong to blame him for all this? Possibly, but he was a convenient target.

Fuck. Kassidy wasn't answering her phone. Maybe Damon Orr was.

Chris scooped up his cell phone from the dresser where he'd tossed it. He was pretty sure he had Orr's cell phone number in his contacts, and if he didn't, he'd start phoning every damn person he did have the number for until he found someone who did.

He had it. His heart thudding, he touched to screen to dial the number. He prepared for it to ring unanswered, as Kassidy's had. Terrible images entered his mind, envisioning the two of them in a hotel room together, looking at the call display and laughing and saying, "Ignore it."

Christ. He was being ridiculous.

"Hello?"

Damon answered. Chris sucked in a breath. "Orr? Is that you?"

"Yeah. Hi Chris."

Damon obviously had his name and number in his phone too.

"Is Kassidy with you?" he demanded, not bothering with polite small talk.

"Not anymore. She left a few minutes ago."

"Where are you?"

"Brix. A wine bar on North St. Claire."

"I need to fucking talk to you."

Damon was silent for a second then said, "You need to talk to *me*?"

"Yeah, you." He was going to punch him.

"I gather this isn't about business."

"Good call."

"Fine," Damon said calmly. "I was just gonna leave too. I'll order another drink and wait for you."

Chris shoved his phone into his jeans pocket and tramped down the stairs. He grabbed a light jacket from the closet.

"Where are you going?" Dag asked, now slouched on the couch in front of the television with his beer.

"Out." He slammed the door behind him. Then he paused. Dag was leaving in the morning. Chris closed his eyes, seeing Dag slumped alone on the couch, and exhaled heavily. But he had to deal with Kassidy and fucking Damon Orr. Then he'd be back to deal with Dag.

Dag watched Chris tear out the door. Chris hadn't said hi to him, had uttered that one single word in answer to his question. That was about the extent of the talking they'd done all week, other than their tense discussion about whether to storm the guest room or give Kassidy her space.

Dag drew in a long breath and let it out slowly, trying to make sense of things. His insides felt hollow. Cold.

Now not only was Kassidy pulling away, Chris was too.

For the first time in years, Dag found himself having those old self-doubts, the voice inside him telling him this was what he deserved for being an asshole his whole life, for screwing around and never caring about anyone but himself. That chip on his shoulder he'd thought was gone…wasn't. He didn't deserve a loving relationship with anyone, never mind two people. He'd worried about being a bad father, and this was just proving his fears right. They'd faced challenges in their poly relationship, but never like this, and here it was all falling apart at their first major adversity and he had no clue what to do to fix things.

How the hell had he thought he could ever be a father?

He chugged back the beer.

He wished he knew what Chris and Kassidy were thinking. And feeling. If he understood what was going on in their heads, maybe he had some pathetic hope of making things better. He'd do anything for them.

Maybe it was good that he was leaving in the morning. He'd been worried about leaving them like this, but maybe it was better. Maybe they'd work things out. Or not. But he'd be far away and wouldn't have to see the implosion of their relationship. His gut churned nastily.

Fucking quitter, a voice in his head told him. *You can't give up on them that easily.*

What the hell was he supposed to do? His flight left at ten-thirty tomorrow morning. Neither of them was even here. They were out fucking around doing who knew what. Apparently they didn't even give a shit that he was leaving.

Bitterness filled his mouth and he swallowed it. It burned all the way to his gut.

He needed another beer.

He pulled himself up off the couch, his body heavy. He popped the top off another bottle in the kitchen and carried it upstairs to the bedroom to throw some shit into a suitcase and call it packing.

Chris strode into Brix and looked sharply left to right, trying to find Damon. There the fucker was, sitting at a high table in a corner. Chris walked over and slid onto a stool across from him, lifting his chin. "Hey."

"Hey, Chris. Want a drink? You look like you could use one."

Hell yeah, he wanted a drink, but he didn't intend to stay there long enough for that and he sure as fuck wasn't going to sit and make conversation with this dude. "No, thanks," he said shortly. "I just need a few minutes." He leaned against the table and fixed his gaze on Damon. "Stay the fuck away from Kassidy."

Damon grinned.

What the fuck?

"I have to work with her," Damon said calmly. "Remember?"

"I remember. I mean outside of work. And enough with the late night meetings. People are talking."

Now Damon's eyebrows snapped together. "What?"

"I was informed today that there are rumors going around about you and my wife. That fucking stops *now*."

Damon's eye flickered. "Wife?"

Chris scowled. "Yeah."

"Chris," Damon said slowly. "There's nothing going on between Kassidy and me. Seriously."

Chris's left temple pulsed.

Damon continued. "Wow, if there are rumors, I'm really sorry, man. Honestly. We've had a few late nights, but this week, that was her choice. I'm not making her do it." Then his chin jerked up. "You want the truth?

She was working late to avoid going home to you and Dag."

Damon's words felt like a punch in the gut. *You and Dag*. What did that mean? Chris struggled for wind.

"I'm glad you came rushing in here to warn me off her," Damon added. "Because it shows you still care."

"Of course I still care," Chris snarled. "Why wouldn't I?"

"Sounds like the three of you have been having a rough time lately."

Three of you. Had Kassidy told this ass the true nature of their relationship? And how the hell did he know they were having a rough time?

"Look." Damon leaned his elbows on the table. "Kassidy's really hurting. She's been working too much, not eating enough, avoiding going home to deal with you. I brought her out for a drink because she needed to talk to someone. So we talked. She told me shit. And I'm gonna do you a huge solid and share it with you, even though it wasn't intended for you."

Chris's brain spun. "What? What did she tell you?"

"Losing your baby was hard on all of you, I'm guessing," Damon said quietly. "Kassidy's blaming herself. She feels like she let you and Dag down. She's terrified that you two would be better off without her."

He did know everything about them. Shit. But Kassidy...Christ, no! How could she fucking think that?

But in a way it made sense. That was how she *would* think. She'd be worried about them more than herself, even if it was fucked up. He closed his eyes and let his head drop. "Did she really say that?"

"Yeah. She's worried about a bunch of other crazy shit too. Dag's apparently leaving? Also, she feels guilty about worrying about how the baby would impact her career." Damon narrowed his eyes at him. "She loves you, man. She was pretty clear about that. You and Dag. You assholes better get your shit together. You're lucky to have her, and if you don't, hey—there's nothing between Kassidy and me, but don't think I haven't thought about it."

"Asshole," Chris snapped.

"Yeah. Go ahead and call me that. I'm just calling things like I see them. Your wife is pretty special. But she's completely faithful to you, so don't blame her for any of this. Blame me. That's what you came here for, isn't it?"

Chris rubbed the back of his neck. "Yeah."

Damon shrugged. "I figured that. Whatever. You need a target and it's not Kassidy. But, dude. I just gave you something to work with. For fuck's sake, go talk to her."

"Where is she? Did she go home?"

"That's where she said she was going."

Chris was already off the stool. He paused and met Damon's eyes, keeping his gaze cool but steady. "Thanks. But what I said still goes. Stay away from her."

Damon smile was crooked. "Loud and clear, buddy. Loud and clear."

Chris was walking up the dark street toward his car when his cell phone rang. Immediately hoping it was Kassidy, he whipped it out. His parents.

Great. Fucking great.

10

After taking the wrong bus and nearly getting lost, Kassidy arrived home to find the house dark but the television in the great room on. She cast her eyes around the room but didn't find Dag or Chris. She nibbled her bottom lip as she wandered through the rest of the main floor. Where were they?

She glanced upstairs and set a hand on the big, carved newel post at the bottom. Were they up there? Nobody was coming to see her. Maybe they hadn't even heard her. Maybe they didn't even care she was home.

She climbed the stairs, listening for voices. Their master bedroom door was closed, only a faint line of light beneath it. Muted male voices came from inside the room, then a low laugh.

Her insides clenched hard.

Crap.

She rushed into the guest room where she'd been sleeping the last few nights and quietly closed the door. Her heart thudded. She'd chosen to sleep apart from them. It was what she'd wanted. Now it seemed awful. Alone. Lonely. They were in the bedroom, maybe even making love. Without her. Again. What was happening to them?

Losing the baby had messed up everything. Now Dag

was leaving in the morning with things all whacked between them. A chill gripped her as if the bedroom window was wide open and wind whipped through the room. She rubbed her upper arms, sitting on the side of the bed in the dark room.

She wasn't sure how long she sat there staring into space before she heard the back door slam with a force that made the bedroom door rattle. She started. What…who was that?

Her heart leaped into her throat and she stared at her closed door. Her eyes went wide. Footsteps thudded up the stairs, down the hall and her door swung open. A large, male shape filled the doorway.

Chris.

She instantly recognized his shadowy outline.

Confusion twisted inside her. Wasn't he with Dag?

"Kassidy." He halted just inside the room. "You're home."

"Y-yes."

"Thank fuck. Get your ass off that bed." He stalked over to her and grabbed her hand, pulling her up.

"Wh-whuh…?"

"I'm so fucking pissed right now," he snapped. "At you and Dag. Come on. This is it, Kass. We end this shit now."

He yanked her hand and tugged her behind him as he strode out of the room, across the hall and shoved open their bedroom door.

Dag was walking toward the door, scowling, apparently having heard them. A big suitcase sat on the bed with a jumble of clothes in it. An empty beer bottle lay on the rug. The TV on the wall was on, flickering light across the lamp-lit room.

"What the fuck?" he said. "What's going on?"

"I'm pissed as hell," Chris said again. The air in the room filled with a swell of vibrating heat. He let go of Kassidy's hand and advanced on Dag. "Fucking want to…do this." And he set both hands on Dag's chest and gave him a shove.

Kassidy gasped. "Chris!"

Dag stumbled back a step. "What the hell?"

"Chris," Kassidy repeated. "What are you doing?"

He rounded on her. "Not happy with you either, sweetheart."

Her eyes went wide and her heart beat wildly. "Why?"

He moved closer. "Damon Orr."

Oh.

"What's going on?" Dag clenched his fists and narrowed his eyes at Kassidy, then Chris. "And why the fuck did you shove me like that? I should punch you, asshole."

"Try it." Chris gave him a slitty-eyed look. "I've wanted to punch you all week, ever since that shitty comment about us being better off without the baby."

Kassidy made a choked sound.

Chris sucked in a breath and let it out, his shoulders lowering. "Shit. Okay. Sorry. I lost it. All the way home, I kept thinking about things and getting madder and madder and—"

"Where the hell were you?" Dag demanded. He set his hands on his hips and glared at Chris. "You came in and left without saying anything."

"I was having a chat with Damon Orr."

Kassidy lowered her chin and bugged her eyes out. "What?"

"I called him, since you weren't answering your damn phone again. And that bullshit stops now too."

She blinked. "How did you know I was with him?"

"Everyone knows you were with him," Chris said, a dangerous edge to his voice. "Apparently there are rumors going around at work about you two. All the late nights, closed door meetings, going for drinks and…" His eyes went narrow. "Holding hands with him."

"The fuck!" Dag snarled, straightening to fix a penetrating gaze on her.

Heat rushed through her. "There's nothing between him and me! How could you even think that?"

"I don't think it," Chris confirmed. "But other people do. *That* bullshit also ends now."

A shiver ran over Kassidy's skin at Chris's take-charge dominance. And then something inside her eased a little. As if she'd needed that. She nodded. "We weren't holding hands," she said. "Yes, we worked late. Oh…wait." She bit her lip.

"What?" Chris and Dag growled at the same time.

"I…I told him about the miscarriage. I was upset and I think he did take my hands, just for a minute. But it was nothing. And I ran into Christy right outside the meeting room when I left…she must have seen."

"She did," Chris stated. "And people put two and two together and got 'affair'."

"Oh no." She put her fingers to her lips. "That's not good."

"No, it's not. I really didn't enjoy hearing that."

She pressed her lips together, her heart crawling up her throat. "I'm sorry, Chris. That shouldn't have happened."

He narrowed his eyes at her. "Why'd you tell him you were pregnant? We didn't tell anyone else at work."

She blinked back tears. "Chris."

The harsh lines of his face softened. "It's okay. It's okay. C'mere, sweetheart."

She fought the pressure that built behind her cheekbones, in her chest. "Chris."

"Come here," he repeated and moved toward her. And then she was in his arms, safe, secure, protected…loved. She buried her face into the side of his neck.

"Chris," she sobbed. "I love you."

"I love you too."

Chris shifted and looked at Dag. "Get over here."

Dag stared at him.

"I'm sorry," Chris said. "I love you too. Now get over here."

Dag shook his head and moved to them, and they circled their arms around each other, heads together. "This week has been the worst week of my life."

"Me too," Kassidy whispered.

"Me three. And much as I'm pissed off at you both, I'm just as much to blame."

They stood like that for a few minutes then Dag pulled back. "Let's sit." He tossed his suitcase onto the floor, clothes spilling out of it, then pulled Kassidy to the bed. She climbed on and sat cross legged in the middle of the big bed, and he and Chris joined her.

"Why'd you tell Damon you were pregnant, babe?" Dag asked the question again, quietly.

"I didn't tell him until I miscarried," she said quietly. "I was a wreck and he needed to know why I was bursting into tears at inappropriate times."

She watched them exchange a look heavy with guilt and unease and frustration.

She sighed. "Did you guys ever think at all about how having a baby was going to affect your careers?"

They exchanged glances. "No."

"Of course not. Because you're men. I wanted a baby and I assumed I would do both—work and be a mother. Then I started thinking about how my maternity leave was going to impact the project, and how I was letting people at work down, and what was going to happen when I came back from maternity leave. Men don't have those kinds of pressures."

"Is that why you were working so hard?"

She shrugged. "Partly. But also because there really was a lot to do. And then, this week, I guess I was avoiding coming home because it reminded me of…what we lost. At work, nobody knew. Nobody was asking me if I was okay, or telling me we could try again, or treating me like I was going to shatter. And you guys were all tense and worried." She shifted her legs, bending them and hugging her knees, setting her chin on them.

"Yeah," Chris said fixing his gaze on Dag. "Since we're getting all this shit out. What the fuck did you mean by saying we're better off without the baby?"

Kassidy stared at Dag.

"I didn't say that," Dag said, rubbing between his eyebrows. "Exactly. I wanted to believe that. Life was good before you got pregnant. We were free and having fun. I kept telling myself we'd be fine. We'd just go back to the way things were before. Telling myself I was never cut out to be a dad anyway. That was how I dealt with it, hoping that would make the pain go away."

"Dag," she whispered.

"I know. I'm an idiot."

"No," she said. "You're not. I was having the same kinds of thoughts."

"Shit," Chris said.

"I was. I was thinking what a terrible mother I would have been when I was so worried about my career and how the timing of getting pregnant was so bad."

"That's not being a terrible mother," Chris objected. "That's being realistic about how you're going to balance life as a mother. Of course your career is important to you. What does that say about us, then, when we never even considered that? Neither of us entertained the idea of taking a leave of absence, or quitting our jobs."

"I did."

They both gaped at Dag. He shrugged. "It was a crazy thought, but I was pretty resentful about having to go to Australia when you were pregnant. I thought about selling the business and doing something else."

When he'd sold his first business for millions of dollars, he'd set himself up for life and given himself the luxury of taking his time and doing whatever he wanted with his career. Maybe she'd had crazy thoughts that he didn't really *have* to go to Australia. But he was committed to this new company, Kassidy knew that, and his casual talk of selling it made her heart tumble. "Dag," she said, reaching for his hand.

His strong, warm fingers curled around hers and it felt so good. He looked down at their joined hands and said in a low voice, "You weren't even here. I'm leaving tomorrow morning and neither of you seemed to even care."

"I'm sorry," she whispered. "I was so angry at you for leaving. I know you have to go, and I kept telling myself now I'm not pregnant, there's no reason for you not to go. But still, I felt like you were abandoning us, at such an awful time."

"Kass. I'm not abandoning you. You were pulling away and I felt like you didn't even care if I left."

Her heart squeezed. "I'm sorry."

"I don't want to be away from you for six months," Dag said. "Both of you. Screw it. I'm not leaving."

She frowned. "Dag. You have to."

He exhaled heavily. "I know. But I'm going to move it back a couple of days. I can do that at least. And I'll come home every month. It'll cost a shit ton of money, but whatever. Hey. Why don't you two take some vacation time and come to Australia?"

She bit her lip. "I'm not allowed to take vacation during the project."

"Maybe we could bend some rules," Chris said.

She and Dag now gaped at him. "Mr. Follow the Rules is suggesting we bend them?" Dag said with exaggerated incredulity. "Holy shit."

Chris grinned. "I'm learning there are always exceptions to every rule."

"I could talk to Damon about it."

"I don't want you working with that guy," Chris growled.

"It's fine," Kassidy said. "I told you, there's nothing between us."

"He wants there to be."

She couldn't argue with that. "I know," she admitted. "But he knows there's no way. I was very clear that I love you both." She met Chris's eyes. "You trust me, don't you?"

Their gazes fused. And he nodded. "Yeah." He slid a hand to her jaw, fingers rubbing the side of her neck, his thumb stroking just in front of her ear. "I trust you."

"I only said that about being better off because it hurt so fucking much," Dag said quietly. "It was my way of dealing with it. But I will honestly tell you, Kassidy…if we don't ever try again, I'll be disappointed…but we *will* be fine. We'll be fine no matter what. And I'll still love you. No matter what."

"Me too, sweetheart," Chris said. "No matter what."

"I'm scared," she whispered. "Scared to try again. What if it happens again? I don't know if our relationship could survive another miscarriage."

"Of course it would," Dag said, his voice raw. "We all learned something from this, something we already should have known. For whatever reason, the pain and grief made us all revert back to our old patterns. We know better. Know we have to talk to each other. Share what we're feeling. Trust each other."

"I felt stupid telling you guys what a failure I felt like."

"Christ, Kassidy. You're not a failure." Dag lifted her hand to his mouth and kissed it. "How could you think that?"

"I felt responsible. I felt guilty. I felt…pressure. I'm the one who can give us a baby, and I couldn't do it. I let you both down."

They both fell silent and she studied their faces as they

worked through whatever they were feeling, identical expressions with raised then lowered eyebrows, mouths tightening into straight lines. Then Chris shook his head. "That's bullshit."

She smiled.

"Yeah," Dag agreed. "You didn't let us down, Kass. Nobody knows why these things happen. It's nobody's fault. Shit. You should have talked to us. Even when you think your fears are irrational, you have to tell us, baby. Holding them in just magnifies them. Getting them out in the open takes away their power to control us."

"You're right," she whispered. "So right."

"I'm guilty too," Chris said. "I even knew what I was doing but I couldn't bring myself to say how I felt. Couldn't even admit it to myself. How sad and angry I was. Not only did we lose the baby, I thought I'd lost having my parents back in my life. That was another thing that was wrecking me. Finally, they'd sounded like they cared when we told them you were pregnant. They were happy for us. And when we lost the baby, I thought I'd lost them again too. But it felt so shitty, admitting that. *You* were the one who went through that physically."

Kassidy's lips trembled. She took a few deep breaths, pushing tears back. "Chris. I'm so sorry. I know how huge that was for you. Maybe I didn't realize enough how bad it was for you guys."

"Yeah," Dag said. "Nobody was asking us a hundred times if we were okay."

"And you lost as much as I did," she said softly.

"Yeah. We did."

"I talked to my parents earlier," Chris said. "They called."

Kassidy blinked at him. "Really?"

"They did. To find out how we were doing." He paused. "I never knew it, but my mom miscarried twice before I was born."

"Oh." Kassidy breathed the word.

"Yeah. She knows exactly what we're going through. And so does Dad." He pressed his lips together. "The things he was saying, about how he felt. I've never heard him talk like that. He's such a hard ass. But he does know. He knows exactly how I feel."

"Oh, Chris." Kassidy's heart squeezed.

"It was pretty amazing." He bent his head. "And Mom. I told her we were all having a hard time with this. And she got that too. She said she and Dad struggled too, especially after the second miscarriage. She said hardship like this can either rip us apart or bring us closer together. It's up to us which it is." Chris lifted his head and met her eyes, his burning and intense, then looked at Dag. "And I knew which it was going to be. I had to fight for you both. I'm not letting it rip us apart."

Kassidy's nose stung and her eyes burned.

"Fuck no," Dag rasped. "We're a team, remember? All three of us, always."

"Yes," Kassidy whispered. "A team."

They shifted on the bed, closer. Dag curved his hand around the back of Chris's neck, his other hand still holding Kassidy's.

"She told me some other stuff too," Chris continued. "Mom's pretty smart. She said that healing doesn't mean forgetting Belly Bean. We'll always remember him or her. And we shouldn't feel guilty if we try again. Trying to have another baby isn't replacing Bean."

"I felt like that," Kassidy confessed. "People said to just have another one, like Bean didn't mean anything. But she…or he…did."

"Yeah. He or she did. Meant a lot." Chris kissed her forehead. "But we won't forget. She said she's never forgotten the babies she lost."

"Oh." Kassidy blinked back more tears.

"But she also said not to be afraid to laugh and love and

have fun, because laughter and joy are healing, and celebrating love and finding pieces of happiness where you can doesn't dishonor your loss."

"Your mom is pretty wise," Kassidy choked out.

"Have to agree," Dag said. "Christ, I missed you this week."

"You had Chris. I thought you two were together in here and didn't even care when I came home."

"I was being an idiot," Chris said. "I was pissed off after Dag made that comment about us being better off. I should have called him on it." He grinned. "Maybe we just should have duked it out then and there. If we'd gotten that out then, if we'd just admitted how much we were both hurting, maybe we could have helped you better. Why were you pushing us away, Kass?" He stroked her hair, tugging a strand off her face.

"I don't even know if I can explain it," she said. "I felt smothered. And pressured. I wanted to be alone. At first. I felt like I didn't deserve that kind of care. And I felt so sad. I've never been more sad. I still feel sad." She met their eyes.

"I know. Me too." Chris glanced at Dag, who nodded.

"It's okay to be sad. We lost something precious," Dag said. "We just need to help each other through it."

"I love you," Kassidy whispered.

"Love you too, babe."

"Love both of you," Chris added with a kiss to her hair. Then he tipped her chin up and her face toward him and kissed her mouth, a long, sweet press of their lips together.

Love for him swelled inside her, her heart expanding hard against her breastbone. She reached for him, hand on his waist. As his tongue stroked over her bottom lip, she opened to him and deepened the kiss. Then she pulled back and turned to Dag. He bent his head and touched his lips to hers. "Babe," he murmured.

And then she watched as Chris and Dag turned to face each other, eyeing each other, their eyelids drooping and mouths meeting. They angled their heads for a hard, fierce kiss, Chris's hand coming up to the back of Dag's head, Dag's hand on Chris's shoulder.

As always, the love her men shared was beautiful and she felt ashamed of being jealous when she'd thought the two of them were together without her. There were many times they had sex with each other in twos, not always three. Jealousy had never been part of their equation. Maybe what she'd been feeling was more anger for taking herself out of the equation when it didn't need to be that way.

They shared more kisses, all three of them, long lingering ones with stroking tongues, getting hotter and hungrier. Hands roamed, big hands tugging her silky blouse out of the work trousers she still wore, sliding beneath, leaving trails of tingling heat in their wake, over her back, her stomach, between her breasts. Heat curled deep inside Kassidy. She wanted these men, wanted their touch, outside and inside. She wanted to show them how much she loved them.

"Wanna fuck you, Kassidy," Chris said. "I wanna love you."

"I wanna fuck both of you," Dag said, voice rough. "Let's get you naked."

His fingers worked the buttons of her blouse and Chris undid her narrow belt. Dag pushed off the blouse and paused to sweep her upper body with his gaze. "Kass. So beautiful." He touched the little pink satin bow between her breasts, trailed his fingertips over the inner curve of one breast revealed in the low cut bra. He reached behind her for the fastener of her bra, flicked it open and tugged it away from her, then gently eased her down to her back on the bed.

She looked up at them, her nipples tightened into hard

points, her breasts full and achy. A tingling pull grew between her legs.

Chris continued the work of removing her trousers and panties. When she lay naked before them, he flattened a hand on her stomach and said, "You okay with this, sweetheart? Not too soon?"

"I'm fine," she said. "I want this. So much. I love you both."

Chris and Dag started undressing each other, sharing kisses between removing articles of clothing. Kassidy rolled onto her stomach to watch them, absorbing the sight of them touching and loving each other, both so big and beautiful, Chris's muscles bulkier, his skin golden, Dag leaner and darker.

Chris stroked over Dag's abs, down to his hard cock through his jeans. Dag bent and took one of Chris's nipples in his mouth and sucked, making Chris groan.

As Chris dragged Dag's pants off, along with his boxers, Dag's cock sprang up, stiff and flushed. Enormous. "Yeah," Chris murmured, eyeing it hungrily. He got rid of the last item of clothing and positioned himself between Dag's legs.

"Suck me," Dag murmured.

"I thought you wanted to fuck me."

Kassidy smiled.

"I do. I will. First, want your mouth on me."

Chris smiled too as he lowered his mouth to Dag's cock.

Kassidy's pussy heated to melting temperature, her core tightening at the sight of her men loving on each other. She would never get tired of this. Watching them pleasure each other with masculine hunger and delight. It made her so hot, and it melted her heart.

Chris lazily sucked and licked, pushing Dag's cock up so he could draw his balls into his mouth. Dag pulled his knees up to give Chris better access, guttural noises of pleasure emerging from his throat. "Yeah," Dag murmured. "Wanna fuck your ass. Now."

They moved apart, both of them breathing heavily, eyes dark and lips parted.

"Get on top of her, Chris."

Chris laid a hand on Kassidy's back. "Like this, sweetheart? Or on your back?"

"On my back. I want to see both of you." She scrambled to roll over, eager to have them both.

She loved it when it felt like they were both fucking her, one of them inside her, the other inside the other man. It was so good for all of them, and she loved being face to face with both of them at the same time.

She adjusted a pillow behind her head as Chris rolled too and moved over her. He parted her thighs and she lifted her knees to accommodate him between them. She watched the head of his cock as he slicked it up and down through her slit.

"Soft and wet," Chris murmured, also watching. "So wet. Want me to use a condom, sweetheart?"

Oh. Her breath hitched a little. "Yes," she whispered. "For now." Things were better, but she wasn't quite ready to try again.

Dag handed him a condom and she watched the look they shared, so loving and understanding. Then Chris pushed inside her, inch by aching inch, until he was fully seated in her pussy. He paused, Kassidy's body throbbing around him. She heard Dag opening and closing the bottle of lube. Then he moved behind Chris, who was on wide-spread knees. Dag's hand came around to Chris's abdomen, then slid up to his chest, holding his body close as he pushed inside.

Her gaze moved between their faces, absorbing the look of ecstasy on both, the way Chris's mouth opened and his eyes closed, the way Dag's eyes went heavy-lidded and his jaw tightened. She watched Dag's arm banded around

Chris's chest, watched one of Chris's hands come up to grip Dag's wrist, his other on her waist.

Chris's cock pulsed inside her in response, thickening even more as Dag slowly eased into his ass. Dag's hand slid up to Chris's jaw, pulling his head around so they could kiss, long and wet, their tongues stroking each other.

Kassidy's nipples tingled and her pussy spasmed around the thick flesh inside her. Beautiful. So much beauty. Beauty inside, beauty outside.

Then Dag released Chris and set a hand in the middle of his back, urging him forward. Chris came down over her, weight on his elbows, one arm around the top of her head, the other on her jaw, and he kissed her too.

They began to move together, slowly, Chris sliding in and out of her, Dag picking up the cadence, one hand on Chris's back, the other gripping his hip.

Together. Forever. Three.

She soaked up all the sensation, the emotion on their faces, the feel of them inside her and around her, their scents mingling into the unique fragrance that drove her crazy, the sounds of their pleasure. They didn't coddle her or treat her like she was fragile. They fucked her like she was strong and sexy, female and desirable. But they touched her with gentle worship and looked at her like she was precious and cherished.

Kassidy slipped a hand down between her and Chris to find her clit, pulsing with need. There…there…oh *there*… Her orgasm shot her up and tore her apart, fire exploding between her legs, waves of pleasure rippling from her core right to her fingers and toes.

"Coming," Dag groaned. "Fuck, coming already."

"Me…too…" Chris gasped. "There is it, oh yeah."

She felt Chris's body go taut and still against her. He buried his face in her neck, and Kassidy watched Dag's face as he came, the grimace, the wash of color in his cheeks, the muscles of his chest, arms and abs going rigid and defined.

"I love you," she said on a near sob. "I love you both. So much."

They both made inarticulate grunts of agreement, collapsing together, panting and sweating.

When they'd all resumed normal breathing and nearly normal heart rates, the guys separated carefully from her and each other and went into the bathroom. She rolled to her side and waited, knowing they were cleaning each other up, knowing they'd come back with a warm wash cloth to clean her up and then climb into bed to snuggle her between them. She smiled into the pillow with languorous joy and satisfaction…and relief.

They'd come so close to losing it all. She closed her eyes in a brief moment of thankfulness. They'd all made mistakes. But if they learned from that, they could come through this stronger and better than ever.

Lord knew they needed strength. They still faced challenges, the same challenges ordinary couples faced, but also ones that were unique to their lifestyle. But together…they were strong enough to take on anything.

Epilogue

One year later

"Oh my fucking God!" Kassidy gripped Dag's arm, digging her fingers into his flesh. Her other hand wrapped around Chris's forearm and she did an ab curl on the bed, panting. Perspiration dampened her hairline, her cheeks were flushed and she'd never looked more beautiful.

Then her fingernails bit into him. Dag winced. "Christ, Kass," he muttered. "You're hurting me."

She turned wild eyes on him. "I'm hurting you? *I'm* hurting *you*? Are fucking kidding me, you sonofabitch?"

"Calm down, sweetheart," Chris soothed, stroking her hair. "Calm down."

She flopped down on the bed. "God, oh God. I can't do this."

"Another contraction," Dr. Fortney said from between Kassidy's spread and raised legs, draped with a sheet. "Get ready to push."

"I can't," she whimpered. "I can't do it anymore."

"Yes, you can, babe." Dag bent and pressed his lips to her damp forehead. "Yes, you can. Sorry about that comment. I know you're hurting. You're working so hard. You're doing great."

"You're a fucking superhero," Chris said, earning a chuckle from the doctor. "No shit. No man is strong enough for this."

"Why?" she whimpered. "Why can't we just lay eggs? It'd be so much easier."

The doctor and nurses all laughed uproariously at that one. What the fuck? Lay eggs? Those were good drugs they'd given her.

Dag helped Kassidy lift her head to roll up and push again. Her face scrunched up, she pushed, breathed, pushed, breathed, then fell back down with a long groan.

"Fuck," she said. Dag and Chris shared a strained smile across the bed. She let out a long exhalation. "What's the score of the game?"

Dag checked the TV screen in the birthing room where the Chicago Blackhawks game played. Kassidy had been using it to focus on as she breathed through the most intense contractions, before she'd been fully dilated and got the urge to push. "Hawks three, Maple Leafs two."

"Good. Ah shit. Here we go again." She grunted and mangled his arm and pushed with what appeared to be everything she had, making harsh, gut-wrenching noises.

"There's the head," Dr. Fortney announced. "Good girl, Kassidy. Next push should do it."

"Oh God," she whispered. She closed her eyes. "I need a minute. Oh shit. Here it comes."

She labored again. Dag wished he could do this for her, take the pain, help in some way other than letting her scratch him and bruise him and curse him. He met Chris's eyes and knew he felt the same. Thank fuck he had Chris there with him.

Nearly there. Nearly there.

"Love you, Kass." He held her hand again, ready for her to crush his bones. Yep. Fucking hell, that hurt. She was strong. Superhero strength, yeah, Chris was right. But no way was his pain anywhere close to what she'd endured. He'd get down on his knees and worship her for the rest of his life for doing this for them. For their baby.

"Shoulders," the doctor said. "Almost there."

"You said that last time!" Kassidy yelled, almost sobbing. "You lied!"

Dr. Fortney's lips twitched. "Yeah, sorry about that. Okay, this time, this'll be it. Come on, Kass, give it your all."

"I can't, I can't."

"Babe," Dag said, hand on her forehead. "This is it. We're about to meet our baby. One more push."

She groaned and when the next urge came, she bore down, chin to her chest. And with that, she delivered their baby.

"Here she is," Dr. Fortney said. "A girl."

Kassidy lifted her head, sucking wind. "Is she okay?" she demanded.

"She's perfect," Dr. Fortney said. "Beautiful. Who's cutting the cord?"

Chris stepped forward, going a little pale. They'd agreed to this before as part of their birthing plan. Actually, they'd flipped a coin. But Dag would get to cut the cord of their next baby.

Assuming Kassidy forgot how bad this was and agreed to have another one. Or to ever have sex again. Apparently memory of the pain would fade due to some hormonal bullshit, although Dag really didn't see how that was going to happen.

She'd been in labor for twelve hours and had pushed for nearly two. She had to be exhausted.

"Congratulations," Dr. Fortney said with a smile at all three of them. "You all did great."

"Blood pressure's dropping," the nurse told Dr. Fortney.

The doctor's attention snapped back to Kassidy. "There was some tearing," she said. "She's losing blood."

Alarm heated Dag's veins at these words. He looked away from the baby to Kass, who'd gone waxy pale. Jesus Christ. He reached for her hand again. "Kass. You okay, baby?"

"Yeah, I'm fine." She smiled at him, her eyes hazy.

"Hang in there, Kassidy," Dr. Fortney said. "I'm going to put in a few stitches."

Chris rejoined them at the bedside, leaving the baby with a nurse across the room to get cleaned up and have Apgar scores done. Dag kept looking over there, worried about the baby, but also worried about Kassidy. What was happening?

"Eight pounds, five ounces," a nurse called from across the room. "Good job, Mom."

"Jesus," Dag said. "Bigger than we expected."

"Healthy baby," the nurse responded cheerfully.

The doctor and nurses worked efficiently, giving Kassidy something to numb her, stitching her up. She was so brave, smiling and trying to look at the baby. When the baby started to cry in short squalls, she asked again, "Is she okay?"

"She's fine," the nurse called. "Good lungs."

"Does that hurt, babe?" Dag asked, nervously glancing back at the doctor working between Kassidy's legs on precious territory.

"Are you kidding me?" She laughed. "After what I just went through? Ha. Nothing will ever hurt again."

"High pain threshold," Dr. Fortney said under her breath. "There. Done."

"Would you like to nurse the baby now?" one of the nurses asked.

Kassidy bit her lip and looked shy but nodded. The nurse helped her get her gown off and another nurse handed her the baby, now swaddled up tight in a flannel blanket. She looked like a burrito. Her little face was rosy and scrunched, with a puff of brown hair atop her head, and she was absolutely fucking beautiful.

"What are you naming her?" the nurse asked.

Kassidy looked up at him and Chris. Her eyes glowed with emotion. "Trinity. Trinity Hope."

The names they'd agreed on if the baby was a girl. They'd waited until she was born to learn whether they were having a son or a daughter. Dag's chest burned.

"That's a lovely name."

Trinity opened her tiny mouth, turned her face into Kassidy's breast and latched on.

"She knows what she's doing," the nurse said approvingly.

Dag watched, dazed, as Kassidy gazed down at Trinity's face, touching her cheek with her fingertips, then gently easing the blanket away from Trinity's chin. When she looked up at him and Chris, standing side by side, her eyes were wet.

"She's so beautiful," she whispered.

Dag's own eyes stung and he pinched the bridge of his nose briefly. Chris's arm came around him. He slid his around Chris's waist and they shifted closer.

Beautiful.

Chris's phone buzzed in his pocket and he pulled it out. "They all want to know what's happening."

"They all" were Kassidy's parents and Chris's parents, who were out in a waiting room. He'd been updating not only them but their friends and Hailey with text messages using a list he'd created ahead of time for this purpose.

"I don't want to leave," he said, worried about

Kassidy's blood pressure dropping and how pale she'd gone. "Wanna make sure you're okay."

"She'll be okay," the nurse said. "She's lost quite a bit of blood, so she's going to need to rest. We'll keep her here a bit to monitor things."

"Are you sure?" He gave the nurse a hard look.

She smiled and nodded. "I'm sure."

"Okay. I'll go tell them. Be right back." He bent and kissed Kassidy's forehead. "Love you."

She smiled beatifically at him.

He left the birthing room and took a deep breath. Wow.

He needed a minute. He paused and leaned against a wall in the hall. His lungs burned as he breathed air into them, his chest full of emotion.

They had a baby. A real, live, crying, eating, pooping baby. Holy shit.

The whole experience was surreal. The pain Kassidy had endured, what her body had been through to bring this new little life into the world was beyond amazing. The relief at the baby arriving safely and Kassidy making it through that swept over him and almost took his knees out.

Okay. Okay. He could do this. He straightened and squared his shoulders and went to find his family.

"Chris!" His mom jumped up seeing him. "What's happening?"

All heads whipped around to look at him.

He grinned. "It's a girl."

They all broke out in a babble, rushing at him.

"A girl," Hope sobbed. "Oh my God. A baby girl."

Dave and Dad stood back a bit, beaming while Chris hugged his mom and Hope.

"Tell us everything," Hope demanded, sounding just like Kassidy. "Are they both okay?"

"They're both fine. The baby is perfect. Eight pounds, five ounces, good lungs, perfect Apgar scores." He couldn't stop the smile that probably stretched from ear to ear. "Kassidy lost quite a bit of blood, so she's a little weak. They're keeping an eye on her, but when I left she was nursing the baby."

"Oh." Hope's eyes filled with tears. "Oh thank God. I mean, I wasn't worried, but…I mean, you always are a little, until…you know."

Mom smiled and touched Hope's shoulder. "We know."

Mom and Dad had arrived a couple of days before Kassidy's due date, hoping to be there when the baby arrived. Although Trinity had taken her time and showed up a week late, they'd been able to stay until she was born. During this time, they'd gotten together with Kassidy's parents numerous times, and the two moms had bonded over their shared grandchild.

Even Dad and Dave had gotten along.

And Chris and Dad had had a talk. A somewhat painful, but profoundly moving talk.

Chris had been surprised when his parents had kept in touch after Kassidy's miscarriage, following up to see how they were doing. When he'd found out about his mom's miscarriages and what they'd gone through, it had forged a new kind of connection between them. The advice his mom had given him had been exactly what he'd needed to step up and deal with what had nearly torn them apart. And when Kassidy had gotten pregnant again, Mom and Dad had been relieved and thrilled for them again.

When they'd arrived to stay with them before the baby arrived, Dad had taken him aside and said, "Listen, I, uh, need to say something."

"What, Dad?"

"I'm not sure if I'm ever going to understand…you and Dag." He'd held up a hand. "I don't want you to try to explain it. I'm dealing with it. But can I ask you a favor?"

"Yeah, what?"

"Would you not…could you two not…uh…kiss in front of me?"

Chris didn't think he'd ever seen his father look more uncomfortable, red staining his cheeks, eyes shifting around.

He'd considered various responses to his dad's request. He'd considered telling his dad he'd damn well kiss Dag whenever he wanted. He'd considered telling him to fuck the hell off. But they were there…Mom and Dad, back in his life, ready to be grandparents to his baby. He got how hard this was for Dad. And he'd learned something important from his dad—that, as a father, he would love and accept Trinity for who she was, no matter what. And saving their kisses for private when Dad was around wasn't that big a price to pay for something that important. It wasn't as if he and Dag would make out in front of his parents; Christ, he and *Kassidy* wouldn't make out in front of his parents.

So he'd said quietly, "Sure, Dad."

"Does she have a name?" Mom asked now.

Again he couldn't stop smiling. "Trinity Hope."

They all went silent and then Hope burst into tears and turned into her husband's arms. He hugged her, his eyes looking a little red as well.

Even Mom's eyes went wet. "That's perfect," she whispered. "Absolutely perfect."

Chris had hoped Mom wouldn't be upset about them using Kassidy's mom's name instead of hers, but the three of them had been unanimous on wanting to name the baby that. It just seemed appropriate. Apparently Mom approved.

"I want to get back in there," he said. "Make sure Kass is okay. You all gonna wait and see the baby?"

"Yes!" The two moms spoke as one.

He returned to the birthing room. Kassidy held the baby on the other side now, but a nurse was about to take her. "That was perfect. Your milk will come in the next couple of days. If you feel uncomfortably engorged, we'll get you some hot towels to put on your breasts. And your nipples will get sore. We'll give you some cream to put on them."

Chris met Dag's eyes. He almost laughed at the expression on Dag's face, mostly because he was sure he looked the same. Freaked the hell out. Jesus Christ. Engorged breasts and sore nipples? What had they done to Kassidy? She was never going to forgive them for this.

But she was nodding, calmly accepting what the nurse told her, having already read up on all this, ready to do whatever she needed to do to be a mom.

"I told the folks," Chris said. "The grandmas are crying."

Kassidy smiled, a slow, tired but beautiful smile.

"They want to see the baby."

"Okay. I'm going to have to stay in the hospital for a few days, because of the blood I lost."

He nodded. "That's good."

She frowned. "How is that good? I want to come home."

"Sweetheart, we want you looked after. We need to make sure you're all strong and healthy when you come home. We'll be here with you."

"You don't have stay every minute," she protested softly. With Trinity now in a tiny clear crib at the foot of the bed, she reached for both their hands. "Thank you for being with me through all this."

"Christ," Dag said. "Where else would we be?"

"I had tickets for the game tonight," Chris said. "Someone at work offered them to me. Could've been there."

They all laughed.

"You are so amazing, Kassidy," Chris said, lifting her hand to kiss it. "I don't even know what to say. I love you so much and I'm so proud of you. Thank you for giving us a beautiful daughter."

"Yeah, what he said," Dag said gruffly. "Love you too. I can't even..." He stopped, obviously choked up.

She gave a watery smile, her bottom lip quivering a bit. "I love you both too. Thank *you* for giving us a beautiful daughter. You had a part in it too."

Later, when she'd been moved to the private room Dag insisted on, along with Trinity in her little bassinette, Kassidy sat with the bed raised, propped on pillows. She felt a little more human with her face washed, her hair brushed and some lip gloss on lips that had gotten dry and chapped, and prepared for her family to meet Trinity.

She was so tired, a little sore, but the incredible relief after all that pain—not to mention some excellent painkillers—made her also feel serene and happy. She'd been told to stay in bed, but she wanted to pick up Trinity. She studied the sleeping baby and was considering slipping out of bed to get her when Dag and Chris arrived.

"Oh yay, you're here." She beamed at them. "Can one of you bring Trinity to me?"

Dag peered around a vase holding what had to be three dozen pink roses. Holy crap. "Chris'll bring her."

"Uh..." Chris nervously eyed the baby. "You want me to pick her up?"

Kassidy laughed. "That's right, Dad. You're not afraid of her, are you?"

"Hell no." But he didn't move toward her.

"Chris! Pick her up!"

"If you're afraid of her now, wait until she's a teenager," Dag said with a smirk. He set the flowers on the window ledge. "These are from both of us."

"They're gorgeous. And extravagant. Thank you so much." The scent of roses filled the hospital room. The sweetness of the gesture touched her way down deep inside.

"You deserve them," Dag said.

She smiled.

"Oh for fuck's sake," Dag said, moving to the bassinette where Chris hovered. "Here." He reached into the little crib and lifted Trinity. He held her confidently but gently. Reverently. She was a good-size newborn but in his big hands she was tiny. He smiled down at her. "Hello, gorgeous."

Trinity opened her eyes and stared right into his, alert as anything.

Kassidy grinned. There was Dag, the charming bad boy no woman could resist. Including his daughter. This was going to be fun.

"Give her to me," Chris demanded.

"Nuh-uh," Dag said, shifting away. "I got her first."

"*I* wanted her," Kassidy said, but her heart was expanding into warm softness in her chest.

"Hello!" Mom's voice from the doorway had Kassidy's head turning.

"Mom! Hi!"

"Kassie!" Mom came at her, bent and hugged her. "How are you?"

"I'm okay. Tired. But good."

"Where's Trinity?" Mom turned. "There she is."

The room filled with people—Dad, Kathy, Hub and Hailey.

Dag moved to show off the now bright-eyed baby.

"Isn't she beautiful?" Kassidy asked.

Everyone agreed, circling around Dag. Then Dag said, "Here, Chris. Your turn."

The two men made heavy eye contact as they did the exchange, sharing a very personal and private smile. Chris looked down at the little bundle in his arms, and she stared up at him too, as if fascinated. She blinked a couple of times, yawned, then her face scrunched up and she let out a long squawk.

"Uh-oh," Chris said. He grimaced. "She needs you, Kass."

Kassidy smiled and held out her arms. "She could be hungry."

She snuggled Trinity into her, so tightly wrapped she was like a solid little package. "Hey baby," she cooed, touching Trinity's perfect tiny lips. "You hungry, sweetie?"

Trinity's mouth opened and she turned her face into Kassidy's breast again.

"Yup, that's what that means," Mom said. "Do you want us to leave?"

"Um, maybe for a few minutes. I kind of need to get the hang of this."

"We'll be outside. Come on, everyone." Mom herded everyone out.

A nurse bustled in. "Time to nurse?" she asked. "Here, let's get your gown lowered…turn her toward your body…lift your nipple to her mouth. That's it." Trinity latched on again. "She's a natural, isn't she?"

Kassidy nodded proudly, watching her baby nurse. She slid her fingers around Trinity's tiny head. Emotion rushed through her, hot and sweet, a fierce, intense love. At that moment, she knew she would do anything for her child. Anything. There were no words big enough to express her love for her daughter. She looked up at Dag and Chris, also watching, emotion darkening their eyes. Damn. She was going to cry again.

"I already love her so much," she choked out. "She's so special."

"She is," Chris agreed.

"Clearly she has a great future," Dag said. "She's already accomplished so much."

Kassidy and Chris both turned their eyes on him.

"She's made us parents." Dag looked from one to the other, his gaze warm. "She's made us proud, happy parents. And she brought our whole family together—including your mom and dad," he said to Chris. "That's quite an accomplishment for someone a few hours old."

Chris smiled and moved into Dag. Dag hooked an arm around Chris's neck, pulled him in and kissed him. "It is," Chris agreed. "She clearly has an amazing future ahead of her."

"I wonder what she'll be like as a grown-up," Kassidy mused, touching Trinity's soft cheek. "I can't wait to find out."

Thank you so much for reading Reward of Three!

Make sure you're on my mailing list for news about my next releases. If you enjoyed Reward of Three please consider leaving a review at the retailer of your choice or at Goodreads to help other readers find my books.

You can also contact me at info@kellyjamieson.com to tell me what you thought of it or ask me any questions!

Enjoy this sneak peek of another of my ménage stories:

One Wicked Night

by Kelly Jamieson

Why did he keep screwing up his life?

Tyler pushed that thought away to worry about later, right now was for Kaelin and making the most of this chance. He'd foregone this incredible gift ten years ago, tried to do the right thing, although somehow he'd screwed that up too, but this time he was taking it. He'd have to deal with the consequences, but he was taking it.

He licked her mouth, kissed her cheek, her jaw, breathed in that scent of fruit and flower, like green apple and honeysuckle, sweet and delicious. "You smell good," he murmured, nose pressed to her neck, filling himself with that warm and wonderful scent.

He shot a glance down her body and watched Nick lift one of her small feet and kiss it, his eyes closed, mouth open. So fucking hot.

Tyler opened his mouth on the side of Kaelin's neck and gently sucked, then kissed his way lower, over her collarbone and onto the soft flesh below. Her breast brushed his jaw and he forced himself to go slow, to kiss between her breasts. She drew in a sharp breath and arched her back in a silent invitation.

Sweat built on his skin, heat rushed through his body. His dick rubbed against Kaelin's hip through his underwear and he wanted that barrier between them gone. He stripped off his boxer briefs and moved back beside her while Nick moved higher, kissing Kaelin's legs and parting them. The scent of her arousal rose to his nose and his cock twitched hard, blood pulsing through his veins in hot surges.

He lifted his head to gaze down at her, wanting the visual, wanting it all, the taste of her, the smell of her, and then, Christ yeah, the feel of her as he dragged his tongue over a nipple, all tight and hard. She gasped and he licked again, and then took her nipple into his mouth and sucked. It fit perfectly between his tongue and the roof of his mouth and she tasted like warm desire.

"Sweet baby," he mumbled against her flesh. "So damn sweet."

Her body writhed and again Tyler glanced at Nick, his hands now parting Kaelin's thighs, studying her, an absorbed expression on his face. He was about to send her rocketing up, and Tyler's body tightened even more. He cupped Kaelin's other breast and gently squeezed, resumed his suckling, then found her other nipple with his fingers and tugged.

She cried out and her pleasure sent a flash of fire through him. Yeah, he wanted to please her, he wanted Nick to please her, he wanted the two of them to make this so good for her. Because if she was going to risk it all to be bad, it had better be good.

Other Books by Kelly Jamieson

Heller Brothers Hockey
Breakaway
Faceoff
One Man Advantage
Hat Trick
Offside

Love Me
Friends with Benefits
Love Me More
2 Hot 2 Handle
Lost and Found
One Wicked Night
Sweet Deal
Hot Ride
Crazy Ever After
All I Want for Christmas
Sexpresso Night
Irish Sex Fairy
Conference Call
Rigger
You Really Got Me
How Sweet It Is

Power Series
Power Struggle
Power Play
Power Shift

Rule of Three Series
Rule of Three
Rhythm of Three
Reward of Three

San Amaro Singles
With Strings Attached
How to Love
Slammed

Windy City Kink
Sweet Obsession
All Messed Up
Playing Dirty

Three of Hearts

Loving Maddie from A to Z

Brew Crew
Limited Time Offer
No Obligation Required

Aces Hockey
Major Misconduct
Off Limits
Icing
Top Shelf
Back Check
Slap Shot

Last Shot
Body Shot
Hot Shot

Bayard Hockey
Shut Out
Cross Check

Dancing in the Rain

About the Author

Kelly Jamieson is a best-selling author of over forty romance novels and novellas. Her writing has been described as "emotionally complex", "sweet and satisfying" and "blisteringly sexy." She likes coffee (black), wine (mostly white), shoes (high heels) and hockey!

Subscribe to her newsletter for updates about her new books and what's coming up, follow her on Twitter @KellyJamieson or on Facebook, visit her website at www.kellyjamieson.com or contact her at info@kellyjamieson.com.

www.ingramcontent.com/pod-product-compliance
Lightning Source LLC
Chambersburg PA
CBHW050900180626
46814CB00007B/2806

* 9 7 8 1 9 8 8 6 0 0 2 8 4 *